Born in the suburbs of London, Zak Myburgh currently lives in the South West with his parents and younger brother. Since he could remember, he's been telling short stories and has recently taken the opportunity to create and publish his first official book.

To my parents

Zak Myburgh

THE BRIDGE AND THE FLARE

AUSTIN MACAULEY PUBLISHERS™

LONDON * CAMBRIDGE * NEW YORK * SHARJAH

A CIP catalogue record for this title is available from the British Library.

ISBN 9781528997089 (Paperback)
ISBN 9781528997096 (ePub e-book)

www.austinmacauley.com

First Published (2021)
Austin Macauley Publishers Ltd
25 Canada Square
Canary Wharf
London
E14 5LQ

I would like to thank Austin Macauley Publishers for their help throughout the publication process.

Table of Contents

The war is drawing to a gruelling close. The Allied ring of steel pushes up from the depths of defeat towards the downfall of their killers. Even with the inevitable victory not far from sight, there still must be men fighting on in the brutal conditions of the battlefield. Through mud and blood, an ordinary British infantry platoon has no preparation to the horrific experiences that lay in wait. No matter the cost, no matter the sacrifice; from D-Day to the Rhine, only one solemn expression remains: there will be no going back.

1 – Hidden Secrets

"How long left, sir?"
"Until death? Ten minutes…"

*H*e heard the roar of the naval guns as they boomed towards the French land opposite them, smashing into the cliffs and shattering machine gun bunkers to blissful shards of raining embers. The early yet overcast sky lay blanketed in the midst of buzzing allied bombers over the shoreline, fighter pilots slicing through the dense clouds and even a prowling huddle of huge zeppelins. A deafening screech was created as the tremendous battleship pivoted right, steering towards the rumbling mainland.

Flint Mitchell witnessed his body shaking uncalled for. For a moment, his memory, almost rapidly, took him over the haunting events that defined the course of his life. The secret. The moment they were all split apart. The outcome of which resulted in now, two months later, descending down a rig into a landing craft crammed with anxious and eager British and American soldiers, shipped off towards the Sword beach.

"Focus in, Bravo Six, we're nearly there," ordered Sergeant Brighton as he stacked loaded magazines of ammunition into his polished belt.

"It's gonna be kind of hard to do that with a beach full of machine guns a few miles away," muttered Hayden. A few of the other soldiers let out a chuckle; however, others were beginning to understand the dark side of it…

Flint glanced, with an eye burning of salt, towards his right flank at the distant Juno beach, a vast array of tiny Canadian boats landing onto the sand. Drumming gunfire could be heard from the shoreline…horrendous scatters of explosions and grenades.

Most infantry shots were muffled by the screaming of men followed by the frantic bombings of the planes overhead. There were dozens of landing crafts *around just like the one they were about to enter, all packed to the brink with petrified young men. Some experiencing their last seconds…*

17 APRIL

1944

He waited until sunset had arrived. It came quite suddenly, ducking under the horizon in a swift fashion. Flint's uncle, Charles, owned a farm in the quiet countryside of Rostrenen, Western France. Only few lights could be seen at night and his uncle liked it that way; living solitary. Flint and his family came here every year for a few weeks to get out from the crowded and bustling streets of Liverpool.

The chestnut-haired and blue-eyed twenty-year-old heard the noise of the engine from a good distance away. Here in this comfortable house, silence had ruled over, it was only the faint chiming of the Victorian clock in the long, wooden corridor that could be heard. Early spring was coming to a closing end, the thought edging Flint to reluctantly decide to wear a woolly grey sweater with dark brown trousers and gloves, buttoned up and polished. The looming engine was getting increasingly louder and soon it came to a stuttering halt. Flint glanced through the cleaned window and saw his bald-headed uncle along with his father, who wore a grey beret and casual grey clothing, unload what looked like…guns?

His family never had any part in this war…or what he had left of his family, his mother had died in a car accident when he was five and his grandparents had just last year migrated to the USA in fear of German air raids. They had wrecked the city and left thousands dead. On the other hand, his father had survived WWI. He had fought in all three major Ypres conflicts but had been shot in the shoulder and hip in the battle of Passchendaele. Intense surgery had been rushed onto him on the frontlines to save his life; however, the doctors had patched him up as best as they could. It wasn't perfect but it would do. When he finally returned home from the war, he had received no hero's welcome, which had been greatly anticipated by the government. Instead, he ended up homeless for a few months before he found Margaret Johnson, a charity worker who then, years later, became Flint Mitchell's mother. Life had become very different since the funeral of his mother; things became more independent for him as he grew up nervous and meek. It was hard due to it being always just him and his brother alone in their urban home in Liverpool. Sure, he had friends and cousins he could hang out with, but there never really was any older person Flint could look up to apart from his dad. (Who'd rather enjoy time being out with his mates than his own children).

His father was a tricky person to live with from the very start. He wasn't like the other fathers in town who had been to the war. They would normally become alcoholics shortly after and abandon their lives, which they had fought so hard to keep. No, he was much to himself, occasionally meeting up with old comrades and discussing some things or two. What they were? He didn't have the smallest clue. But when Flint was fifteen and when World War II had started, his father had changed his ways with the outside world after he restored contact with his brother, Charles. He was now going to offices and meetings all over Liverpool. And Liverpool's a big place. Much was hidden about him and that made Flint worried.

But what was the reason for him to be carrying two Thompsons through the front door?

Flint swung the beige patterned curtains over and called for his younger brother, Christopher Mitchell, who inherited the bright and bold age of seventeen, who came running down the stairs. He had a round, boyish face with black hair slightly flopping onto his forehead. Christopher was relatively small for his height, but that never stopped him of trying to act the biggest.

"They're carrying—" he muttered in a surprised manner.

"Guns. Yes. I have no idea what it's about, but I'll see if I can figure it out."

"We should ask them!" demanded Christopher. He jogged down the corridor to the front oak door; Flint heard the keys jangle outside and swiftly pulled his brother into the kitchen. Together they heard the door open, it sounded as if there were beers in a bag and their father hurried into the kitchen worryingly.

"All right, leave it here. I think we outdid them," his father's deep voice echoed through the room. Suddenly, Christopher impatiently burst past Flint and caught his dad red-handed.

"Oh! Chris, you gave me a fright!" howled Jonathan Mitchell.

"Why are there guns on the table?" asked the younger son curiously. "And are those grenades?"

Jonathan smirked and calmed himself down by heavy breathing, pulling up a chair elaborated in dense Celtic carvings.

"Take a seat." A sudden chill of seriousness swept over his face like ice.

"You too, Flint," Charles commanded. It was the first time Flint had heard his uncle speak today and anyone could tell that his 'fifteen years of living in

England' accent was gradually starting to be replaced by a French one. It didn't stop him being his old, usual nationalist self though! Flint trod through the doorway and placed himself onto the woolly sofa, listening intently.

"I am about to tell you something I never should have even thought of saying to you before."

"Well, what is it?" Flint remarked.

His father added, "But since you have seen the guns—"

"And grenades," pointed out Christopher. Flint was starting to get irritated with his cheekiness.

"Yes…and grenades." He sighed casually with hints of annoyance. "I figured it's time."

Father hesitated for a few swift seconds.

"German soldiers are hunting us down…more and more by the minute. Why? We work for the British Intelligence Corps FRA."

Flint's heart stopped, all this time since the start of the war, his own father was an intelligence officer for Britain in France.

Intelligence Officer?

A few moments ago, I was just thinking about our family not being involved in the huge conflict, but there my dad goes and wants himself to be some sort of national hero, he thought discretely.

"So…you're like a…spy?" Flint mumbled carefully. "You're fifty!"

"No! Ha ha! Me? Running around Paris with the resistance? I'm a bit old for that, Flint. It's a different sort of intelligence officer. I'm an interrogator for captured axis soldiers, officers, sometimes even politicians." He shrugged. "It's the only way the allies get their information about what's going on here in Rostrenen and even the entire west of France! We have a headquarters fifteen miles south from here."

Flint and Christopher were trying to swallow what had just met their ears.

"Okay…so why are there guns on the table?" Flint nodded at the weapons perched on the oak. "And you said you 'outdid' the Nazis? What's happened?"

"The French resistance kidnapped Stefan Jurgen, a massively powerful Nazi general in Marseille. He was interrogated. But nothing happened. He didn't say one word, even with those Frenchman beating him," Jonathan began sourly. "He was getting shipped over for me to inspect; find something the others couldn't.

But first, we had to go collect him from our allies meaning we had to pick him up in their sector, Gouarec. Locals informed us the only safe-for-resistance bridge across the Le Blavet River had fallen a year ago and had finished being rebuilt today, issuing the transfer of Jurgen to be pushed forward to…today. Well, we must've been double-crossed by the locals, 'cause the bridge was still standing. Aside from that however, it didn't affect us too much. Why they tricked us? We had no idea. We finally met up with the car in a nearby field."

"Still can't believe those French," muttered Charles angrily under his breath.

"Jurgen's previous informers were there and we traded the general. Good, right? But then in the field…lay a dozen Nazis waiting. We only realised that when they shot the informers and started at us."

"We had no choice but to get in the car and go," Charles cut in.

"And?" Flint replied. "Where's Jurgen now?"

"Your uncle shot him whilst driving away. He couldn't be allowed to be recaptured."

Flint and Christopher slowly nodded. Charles smiled under his hands, which covered his mouth. Both brothers were speechless and had nothing to say.

"We've got to go out again, though, and get out of here 'cause they've seen the area in which we headed back. And you're coming with; German's are not the slowest when it comes to finding people." Jonathan chuckled. He then added with a quick glance at Christopher, "If it wasn't for those French locals we wouldn't have to evacuate. Ha." He chuckled again and looked at Charles. "It's like what that senior said to us before we left; 'Betrayal is the loyal one's worst enemy.'"

BANG!

Suddenly, like a punch to the stomach, the door blew open, blasting bits of wood and plaster that scattered into the corridor. Screaming could be heard edging nearer, quickly getting louder and louder.

"Erhebe deine Hande!"

Soldiers wearing grey uniforms and red armbands burst into the kitchen one by one. Their faces moulded into an extremely serious yet satisfied expression. Flint spotted a swastika on almost every single one.

They had come.

The Nazis aimed their rifles straight at Flint's forehead, making sure he and his family made no movements at all. Hundreds of thoughts chased around his head, but all his brain was registering was, '*Beweg dich nicht!*' and '*Ich werde sheiben!*' He had no idea what it meant, but he certainly was not going to ask. Like out of a movie, a tall slender officer casually strolled their way. Flint was still sitting on the woolly sofa, just not so comfortably anymore. The dark, inferior elder walked dressed smartly in a black buttoned-up uniform with a swastika armband and a thin grey striped tie; furthermore, he prided himself with iron crosses strapped all over his chest mixing in with various coloured medals. Flint also did not want to know what they had been achieved for. He had a pair of white gloves, which looked immaculately clean in pellucid pale.

"Are you Jonathan Mitchell?" he spat out with a thick German accent as it rolled delicately off his tongue.

No reply.

He slipped his right glove off his hand and slapped Flint's father straight across the face. A red mark started to slowly appear. Flint felt anger brewing inside of him, a whirlwind of hatred at these people who had committed a world war and had just slapped his dad in front of him.

"Are you Jonathan Mitchell?" he blurted out menacingly once more, this time more similar to a raging, coiled viper about to strike.

A trembling minute passed.

"You! Sit there!" He pointed at Charles out of the blue, his finger dragged to a spot on the sofa next to Flint, which lay empty. Around six guards surrounded them; watching intensely as Charles lifted up and repositioned himself.

"Now with that done, I can speak to the man who is apparently mute. Listen, if you do not respond with me I will give you to the Fuhrer who will personally execute you himself. Is that clear!"

At this moment, Flint witnessed his uncle eye the Thompson gun on the table in front of him. Filled with looming uncertainty, he watched as Charles dug his farmer's boot into the ground below him, like he was preparing for an all-out firefight.

"I am Jonathan Mitchell."

"Good. Come with me!"

"And I wouldn't mind shooting you and your Fuhrer for the animals you are," Flint's father spat into the commander's armband.

The German twisted into a sneer of disgust. It then all happened. Flint knew from the very start it was all a lethal trap his uncle had fell into. What kind of officer would allow a gun to be put right on the table in front of prisoners? That's the reason why that Nazi had ordered Charles to sit next to Flint, so that he could reach the weapon. Within swift, sharp seconds, the officer whipped around with a small handgun; and enjoyed the moment as he watched Charles scramble for the Thompson.

BANG!

Dark red liquid splashed all over Flint's face as his uncle was launched over the sofa, headfirst onto the floor, revealing blood splattered onto the wall behind him. A smirk widened over the officer's face as he lead Flint's father out of the main door onto the crunching gravel driveway. They left Charles' body silently lying on the floor after a few post-death shots to make sure he was long gone.

Suddenly, Jonathan Mitchell's anger was released onto the officer, wildly swinging multiple punches at him. The other guards burst out to help their leader, leaving only one singular soldier between the two gasping brothers.

"Flint, now!" Christopher screamed.

He acted swiftly, launching himself onto the guard and dropping him onto the floor so hard that his back might have broken from the impact. Unfortunately, the soldier managed to bounce back up, slightly winded however still throwing punches aggressively at the rushing older brother. Flint was hit several times in the face, blood streaming from his nose before he tumbled to the floor unsuccessful. Chris rugby-tackled the German to the floor with a mighty smash. A lumbering groan echoed from the clobbering two. Somehow from out of nowhere, the soldier produced a knife from behind his clean yet dark boot and plunged it directly into Christopher's stomach.

"Arghhh…" his voice slowly faded away. Dodging the knife, Flint smacked the object from his hand and slammed his foot into the centre of the soldier's body. The Germans stood still, bending over, wheezing for gulps of precious air. Flint finished him off with a slowly charged uppercut to the chin. The German was flung into the furniture and the cutlery came crashing down on top of him. Motionless, he stared into space as if taking in his last moments of consciousness.

"No, no, no," mumbled Flint as he heaved Christopher into the kitchen.

His brother's breathing was getting notably heavier; the stab wound allowing streams of blood to soak into his clothes. Flint lay him down on the floor next to the window; he then ripped open the upper cabinet and chucked a roll of bandages and a used bottle of morphine at Chris, telling him to apply it.

"Put it on and patch yourself up!" An undeniable tone of urgency could be heard in Flint's voice. "I'm gonna help Father!"

Christopher groaned as if agreeing; and painfully flung the Thompson at Flint.

"Take…it…"

Flint nodded, catching the weapon in mid-air, loading it and sprinting two floors up to the top window in seconds, leaving his suffering brother downstairs with the medicine. Christopher Mitchell crawled towards the table, his wound not getting any better with sweat dripping off his forehead. Pain hit him like a drum when he finally rose up, grabbing the last Thompson and limping out the kitchen door.

Flint was perched on the edge of the window, aiming down the sights, which were locked straight on to the Nazi officer's head. The boy was filled with deep vengeance. He witnessed the fight erupting between that evil man and his dad; however, he could never get a clear shot. He waited until they were split apart, so that he could pick the Germans off without shooting his own father by mistake. Flint froze impatiently still. Fortunately, to his luck, the officer tumbled backwards, dust scattering into his face and eyes, he staggered back up again, blinded for a few vulnerable and precious seconds.

Now.

A gunshot rang out through the farm, piercing the silence and agitating a few nearby ravens. Bewildered greatly, the officer fell to his knees looking down at the hole in his body. He cascaded into the stones. Immediately, the other Germans bolted for cover behind the convoy in which they arrived in, terrified to know there was a shooter nearby. Flint fired rapidly at them, skims of gravel and dirt leaping into the air around the scrambling soldiers.

"*Hol die Bazooka!*" were their cries. Flint instantly knew what it meant and rushed downstairs to escape into the cornfields. *They are going to blow the whole house up!* He thought. But first, he had to rescue his brother and father. He ran into the wooden corridor, the Thompson he had just used strapped across his back. Flint called out for Christopher, but worryingly there were no answers back, only the shrieks raging from on outside. Next, he darted into the kitchen, a blood pool and his uncle were still seeping on the carpet lifelessly however there was no sign of his brother or the…other gun.

BANG! BANG! BANG! BANG!

Deafening gunshots were erupting outside. With the sickening feeling he had, Flint saw Chris lying on the gravel, shooting randomly at the armoured trucks with one hand, bullet's holes opening up in the green bonnet paint. There was a trail of blood smeared behind him.

"Chris!" Flint shrieked.

Christopher's head swung back, noticing Flint calling out for him. But when his eyes looked forward again…he was met with the appearance of a rocket launcher.

"Take cover!" howled Flint.

An immense fireball of heat and destruction swept right past Flint, his body automatically throwing himself out of the way to avoid it. The ageing entrance was blasted to pieces, rocks and debris flying in all directions. Flint glanced up, seeing that they were already reloading the weapon and ready to shoot again without mercy. Christopher was not shaken by the explosion and kept on firing at the dozen Nazis who were left, repeatedly slamming his bullets towards them. One instantly fell and the other cried for a medic. The rubble was heaped upon Flint and ash was choking the back of his throat. His father stumbled towards him and pulled him out of the mess like a hopeful torch in the dark.

"*Feuer!*" one German commanded.

BOOM!

Another rocket skimmed Flint narrowly and created a brutal explosion in the house, fire and smoke engulfing the building. Flames leapt higher into the sky and were silenced by a colossal cracking noise, which could be heard just over Flint's head. Burnt bricks started to drop down from the rotting roof and the entire house suddenly slanted forward, hurling shatters of glass and metal to the floor. Without even the slightest of hesitation, Flint burst away from the building, which was now starting to cascade down, creating an almost tsunami-like effect. Debris came barrelling, pounding into the earth rapidly. Ahead, the Germans were hiding behind their convoy of vehicles again, hoping that no odd brick or glass would hit them where they stood. However, behind Flint, it was a different story. He looked back to see his own father, who had done so much for the world, good or bad, crushed by the tall brick chimney that had come raining down. There was no cry of pain or famous last words. He had been finished in a matter of milliseconds. And then it was all suddenly over. No more crashing down buildings or flying bricks to be hit by. It had stopped just like the snap of a finger.

Like the home behind him, Flint fell to the ground, quickly snatching his gun off his back before starting to slowly crawl forward. He couldn't see Christopher anywhere. This gave him a huge wave of sorrow, which turned into delight as he spotted him creeping up from the polluting dust, panting and coughing. Chris painfully waved Flint over and alerted him.

"Listen, Flint," he said sighing, deeply worried with what he was about to say, "You have to go! I won't be able to make it outta here with the amount of blood I've lost. I'll cover…I'll cover you so you can escape—"

"No! Never! Are you out of your mind?" Flint demanded. He now noticed that Christopher's wound was spilling out more blood than before.

"You have to! There's a HQ fifteen miles from here, just like…" he began to stutter, choking on his own short breaths, "…just like Father said. Go there and you'll be…safe. Leave me…" His nose was starting to bleed, he realised that while he was swallowing a gulp of air slowly. Christopher's hair was now dripping with sweat, he looked battered and increasingly pale.

"I can't! We can fight them together I know we ca—!"

"NO! You have to go!"

BOOM!

A rumbling explosion vibrated the very earth around them as a menacing red cloud of dust launched into the clouds. Scatters of metal and bricks rained down from the sky.

"Arghh!"

Flint shook the ash from his hair and glanced at his groaning brother. It was the worst sight he would ever want to see. A bullet had zipped through his chest and splattered blood all over the rubble.

"No!" Flint howled in agony whilst trying to stop the bleeding.

"Go!" Chris shouted as he clambered upon one of the brick heaps next to him and positioned himself so that his Thompson was facing the Germans. Flint lost into a trance…before nodding with deep regret and signalling his brother. From then on, his human instinct was in control…not his heart. It was just him fighting for survival despite the unbearable consequences.

The Germans now were slowly starting to exit their hiding places, crouching down whilst manoeuvring and cautiously aiming at everything that so much inched. They wandered as a pack, heading towards the brick heaps where the brothers were and now around five metres away. They had no idea what was about to hit them.

"Do it," whispered Flint, holding back the tears.

RATATATA!

Christopher shot two of the Germans within the first second; he was spraying the lead over them without the slightest intention of mercy. Why should he, a dead man, care to kill such monsters? Christopher saw one of them try and make their way back behind cover; however, he shot him diagonally through the arm. Blood spurted out and the German tumbled to one side.

"GO!" shouted Christopher, the words had caused him a great deal of pain to say, but it was the last words he probably would ever say anyway.

Flint ran.

And there Christopher Mitchell stayed with no fear of what would or could happen. One…two…three…four…five and counting. Germans were gunned down in the midst of the chaos as they gradually gained ground on him, until one rifleman managed to shoot him straight through the shoulder. He lay dead there for days, tangled in a mess of debris. But they had pulled it off. Flint was out of sight before anyone realised he was gone. And through the cornfields and farmlands and past ploughs, he ran.

He had one destination and one only.

British HQ Rostrenen.

2 – Foreign Showdown

He had managed to locate it, burrowed under an abandoned shed at the edge of the overgrown evergreen. It had various weeds, bushes and rose shrubs spewing out the sides with vines rooting it to the spot, as if wanting it to stay where it grew. The colour mixes of dark green, brown and grey made it hardly attractive at all. At first glance, anybody might have thought it was left to rot decades ago, but if you dive deeper in, say you removed the rusting metal floorboards, you would discover an organisation teeming with human life. Computers, telephones, desks and workers were all in this underground base. It was specially designed to look for it never to be investigated and that it was increasingly ancient. The fact is that it was made only at the start of the war, five years ago, and with the help of the intelligence agencies, it looked nothing like it.

It was actually quite an accident that he stumbled upon it. The night was melting in and Flint had no ideal shelter for the next twelve hours, so he pitched himself inside the small roof and wanted to slowly drift to sleep, but it never came. The tragic events of the day had shaken him too much; it was all too quick. His father's death and leaving his younger brother behind and witnessing his uncle shot right next to him and the house cascading down…it was horrible. But somehow, gradually, he could hear voices around him. He peeked into the dark forest behind, but there were no figures to be seen in the shadows. Voices echoed from beneath him. Confused, Flint thought it must have been some homeless people in a train tunnel, but why would there be a train underground cutting through the countryside? Fumbling with the floorboards, he found an edge that he could lift to enter and heaved the metal boards up, carefully leaving them on the side just next to the spiralling vines. He was met with a gentle funnel of light, which poured into the wilderness and spotted the rusting brown ladder leading down; he put a foot on the top rusting bar and plunged in.

All sorts of electronic devices met his eyes: calculators, computers and radios were all being used by the dozens of people that inhabited the place. The complex was created out of cobblestone and limestone that were rotting in some corners, but it did have bending walls and singular offices, which riddled this maze. More than fifty desks all pointed towards the main television screen; a lone projector could be seen attached to the roof, light strobes providing the television screen with military planning content. Cables infested the place; around ten exiting from each desk, the sheer complexity of this place amazed yet completely surprised Flint. *All this from an abandoned shed?* He thought. Almost at once, Flint found himself surrounded by soldiers in combat overalls, pointing handguns at him and shouting commands, which Flint obeyed instantly. The guns they aimed at him were the standard issue Webley Revolver for the United Kingdom's forces, short and stubby but more powerful than anything. He was rushed to his knees, held down in case of an attack and violently pinned to the concrete. Flint found himself staring into the bright lights on the roof shimmering down on his eyes, ignoring the fact that he was at gunpoint.

"Who sent you!" cried one of the guards; he had a small nose and chubby chin and looked quite young with his flicked black hair, probably one of the new fresh-faced recruits. A badge was pinned on his chest reading 'Stephens'. He certainly had an Irish accent to add onto the name.

"I…I…" Flint was too stunned to speak, dazed by the sudden amount of weapons inches from his head.

"I said, who sent you?" shouted Stephens again. He cocked his revolver right in front of Flint's eyes.

"Jonathan Mitchell, my father, he worked here!" reassured Flint, trying to calm him down.

"Yeah, paired up with his brother, um…Charlie, that's it, why did they send you here then?" replied a radio operator behind Stephens.

"They're both dead. Same as my brother. Nazis arrived at our doorstep."

"How do I know you're not a spy, ay? Tryin' to mislead us right into some forsaken ambush."

"I wouldn't, I'm Engl—"

"Okay, Stephens, we get it now."

The stern sentence had come from a tall, slim man who had deep brown eyes and the same coloured hair. Well-built in muscle, it was obvious he had been in conflict before as his eyes looked as if they had seen too much. A horrible scar stretched across the left side of his neck. It looked as if a bullet had been dragged past it in brutal fashion.

"You think just because you've achieved second lieutenant you're allowed to take the lead around here? But if you want to get discharged or demoted back to private…go ahead, be my guest," demanded the officer. He was keeping his voice down, but it still sounded intriguingly rough. Stephens took a step back and coughed twice to break the awkward silence, it had seemed like Flint had been very much forgotten.

"Your name is?" asked the officer, nodding at Flint. Never mind.

"Flint Mitchell."

"Good. Know me as Sergeant Brighton. And your family has been killed by a Nazi raid?"

"Yes, sir," Flint replied.

"Stephens, the documents, please."

Stephens scurried over to his sergeant and cautiously handed over a thick slab of aging papers. Brighton sternly glanced over at Flint, who was standing up now, before licking his fingers and opening up the document. The other members of the squad watched as Brighton scanned the page for a few seconds before raising his eyebrows and reading what was stated.

"Flint Mitchell, nineteen, last seen Dover, ferry across to France, alive. Relatives: Charlie Mitchell, fifty-seven, uncle, ex-RAF pilot in WWI, works for HQ Rostrenen, interrogation officer, last seen at Rostrenen. KIA. Jonathan Mitchell, sixty-two, father, ex-colonel of British 5th Army in WWI, works for HQ Rostrenen, interrogation officer. Last seen at Rostrenen. KIA."

"How do you know all that?" asked Flint, gobsmacked that all his relatives' information had been recorded and printed into a document specifically for them.

"We're the biggest HQ in South West France! I think we know what our workers are doing. Anyway, we keep an eye on our friends." Sergeant Brighton grinned.

"What now?"

"Technically, you're not allowed in here without being authorised personnel, so we will have to take you to the nearest refugee centre, which is in Locmaria, east of here. There is one other option however, and to be honest, I think that's your only hope to avoid sleeping rough for the next few weeks."

"And that is?" Flint muttered back.

"Enlist."

Flint was mightily shocked and rather taken aback.

Brighton had just recommended for him to join the war. A world war. For a moment, Flint was telling himself that he must be delusional to even be thinking of agreeing to it. He shuddered at the very thought. However, there was the tiniest part of him that secretly rebelled to this; something had snapped inside of him since his entire family's death and he sought revenge. He had nowhere to go. Nowhere to live. He would become homeless in a couple of months even if he did succeed in getting back to England. Flint would do it for his family, for the millions of other families ripped apart by the forces of this world who were affected by the Nazi regime. He wanted to help.

"All right, I'll join," Flint said, wondering whether he would end up regretting…or if it would be too late. Brighton nodded casually and then escorted Flint towards the enlisting station.

The sergeant smiled as he watched Flint tagging on close behind. It was one of those classic enlistees ready to 'destroy the German war machine' and 'liberate the civilians'. He knew it all too well. They were the sort to perish in the opening seconds. He smirked once more. Like Flint really knew the horrors that would come his way.

They occasionally hopped over the tangled wires leading out from the underside of the desks. Flint took in the atmosphere as he walked, dull female workers with typewriters or telephones in their hand busily gathering foreign intelligence, generals commanding a group of standing new and eager recruits what to do; and of course, soldiers without helmets playing darts in one of the sleeping areas.

"Hi, I'm Anthony Walker, deputy head of the enlisting here in Rostrenen. Name?"

He was one of the first cheerful-faced members, probably trying to avoid them thinking they would be sent to northern France for ultimately certain death. He was bald, middle-aged and there was another Webley Revolver hooked onto his belt next a platinum keychain.

"Flint Mitchell," he replied.

Flint waited a few minutes until Walker had made all the signatures. It was all a bit too quick. He asked whilst keeping an eye on the deputy head, "Where is my unit, sir?"

"Right here, Mitchell, you're now part of British 3rd Infantry Division, you'll be shipped back to England in a few days. Allied forces are planning an invasion of Normandy in a month or so. You're up. First, though, here's the list of your comrades." Walker handed Flint a clipboard and he scanned it through thoroughly.

British 3rd Infantry Division: Delta Company: Bravo Six

Pvt. Luka Smith	Pvt. Harry Willis
Pvt. Hayden Hendrix	Pvt. Jack Harper
Pvt. Ruben Cruz	Pvt. Flint Mitchell
Lt. Stephen O'Leary	Lt. Alexander Cole
Sgt. William Brighton	

"All your supplies are in the main storage unit in Bunker Room Seven. Along with your M1 Garand. Germans cut British supply routes across the channel last week so we're stacking up on American weapons. Not the same effect but it'll do!" He chuckled. "Good luck, private."

Flint walked over to the main storage unit and introduced himself to his first comrade, Jack Harper, who was smoking by the wall in the corner. Jack was a very short yet stocky person, muscles bulging out of the sleeves; obviously, he had been to the gym for many hours. He had army-style short hair, nearly bald and a smug face. Flint found him to be quite the arrogant type, always being the head of celebrations or parties but not having any actual common sense. Sort of like his brother. Flint painfully now remembered the ordeal with the Nazis, which led Christopher sacrificing himself for him. It was the Nazis he had come to fight and so it would end there just like it ended with his brother. In the palms of the Germans.

Flint saw himself out, grabbing the heavy M1 Garand and ammo before heading into the area where the rest of the men played darts. He had used the M1 Garand a few years ago in the vague woodland in the English countryside; his father had commented that he had quite a shot on him, that Flint was much better than his lads in the trenches. How could the thought of shooting a squirrel from fifty metres away turn into a person at ten? Flint calmly walked to the other soldiers, his rifle hanging down from his back, hoping that it would be a different first impression on the rest of them.

"Flint, right? Welcome. I see you've made it to the third!"

It was Hayden speaking. He was a relaxed, thoughtful individual with an athletic build and short blonde hair with a fringe on top. He was the sort of person who was loyal and focussed on sticking together. Around the same age as Flint, they became friends gradually over the next few weeks in basic training, shooting at the firing range and being on camp together.

"You're the last one to join! A bit late but better than never. Where do you come from, mate?"

"Liverpool, Sandfield Park," Flint replied.

"I had a friend up in Sandfield, a baker, nice guy but we've lost contact over the years. Something about his family and the Blitz."

Flint nodded and curiously asked, "What do you work as?"

Hayden paused for a brief second before remarking, "I nearly forgot! It's been so long! I run a trading market up in Manchester, some Herb factory or something; we've stretched across most of England and Wales. Even thinking about Ireland! Good job, I do travel a lot to other European countries, I guess. Shame you can't anymore. All you would see is Hitler's face on every poster. But anyway, since this war has broken out we've had a lot of time on our hands. Me and my sister, name's Helena by the way, have been living well even with our city being called into red alert. Times have changed."

Flint also discovered a lot about the other comrades as well. Harry was a maths teacher in Lancashire, giving up his career to serve as a trained medic. Also, there was Luka Smith, an architect from Manchester who prided himself in works throughout now Nazi-occupied Helsinki. Furthermore, Ruben Cruz was a typical Portuguese tour guide but joined to try and stop the Spanish taking over; the other soldiers weren't sure if he had signed up for the right army! Stephen O'Leary was named as the Irish version of Jack even though it was worthless how many times he tried to deny it. Other fellows just knew him as old 'Stephens'.

On the other hand, in vile contest, with the leaders up front, you could tell there definitely was an edgy relationship between Cole and Brighton. Both had fought alongside one another in Burma. However, due to very different opinions, rumour has it that they were split up in an ambush and forced to retreat from a key port that took the allies months to claim.

He liked his platoon. It was just interesting now to see how they would work together in a war zone…

3 – Sinking Feeling

After their stay at Rostrenen, they travelled by battleship on 29 May to Dover, the captain and crew of the ship were extremely wary of any mishap or odd wave in the water. There had been numerous reports of German U-Boats sinking all kinds of shipping devices leaving England. Cruisers, civilian transporters, battleships and allied submarines had all been slain victims to the 'Invisible Death' as the Royal Navy liked to call them.

"Flint? I got you this. Just so you don't end up like James."

Flint looked up from his cafe seat to find Hayden casually moving towards him, holding two bottles of water in his hand. He could also make out James, the medic, in the background leaning next to an empty oil barrel, sick flowing out of his mouth.

"Thanks," spoke Flint as he caught the bottle, which Hayden threw to him and sipped quickly.

He then started to walk away but then turned around and asked, "Are you worried?" asked Hayden, Flint could tell that him getting nearer to the war had made him more queasy every minute.

"Nah, not entirely, anyway with you and the others together with me I feel much safer. Because there are more people for the Nazis to aim at." Flint laughed when he said it and Hayden did too reluctantly whilst heading over to Alexander and Ruben.

Flint became increasingly bored and strutted to the main deck, eager to look at their progress himself. He could feel the lapping of the waves onto the surface of the ship and the whistling wind bustling outside. He passed the toilets then the bunks, which he had left his rifle in, to finally walk onto the main deck. At once, the sea salt came spraying over into him, diving into his face and clothes. Flint clung onto the metal railings to stabilise himself from the rocking ship, glancing down to see huge waves ten metres down smack into the hull, over and over again they came. It was a miserably overcast day with clouds gathering immensely to form gale force winds, with bleak unsettling waters stirring beneath. His dark green trousers flapped wildly and Flint staggered over to the centre top deck of the ship, met by the sight of strained crewmembers either huddling together or carrying supplies from one end to the other, occasionally shouting muffled commands. Their faces were damp and drained, exhausted from having to do such manual labour loads in these conditions. From out of the blue, multiple dark objects could be seen in the sky many miles away, growing larger in size as they approached. Soon after, droning engines could be heard. It reminded him faintly of when his dad was coming back to the house from the farm. The sort of desolate quietness, which then greatly erupts. Bewildered, Flint sprinted over to one of the officers on deck that had a pair of binoculars lazily hanging down from his chest.

"Sir!" Flint called and saluted, he was met by an unwelcoming face, but one who could most likely help. His name was Peter Chambers, as stated by his navy badge.

"Yes, private, what is it?" Chambers gloomily replied, acknowledging that this was just another inexperienced soldier seeking for attention. He was middle-aged and had an exquisitely posh English accent, probably living somewhere in Windsor.

"Over there, in the distance, those airplanes. Are they ours?" Flint questioned. The navy officer couldn't be bothered to lift up his head.

"Listen, private, if you have any concerns or 'queries', please leave it with someone with the ability to help. Go and ask one of your 'army generals' to aid you or something. You soldiers are good at that; begging for help."

"Soldiers are forced t—"

"Shush, shush. We've all heard it before," interrupted Chambers, soured by the reply. Flint couldn't believe how against his own people this man was. What kind of smug person was he? He acted swiftly, ripping the binoculars of its string and peering through the glass.

"Excuse me!" Chambers shouted, clearly disturbed by this random man snatching his binoculars. He awkwardly barged Flint hard in the stomach, toppling him over and making him drop the object. Flint's helmet also fell off, spinning around on its top.

"I shall report you to the Army Discipline Court! You deserve four years, lower-class scum!" shouted Chambers. He knelt down slowly, grabbing his binoculars and staggered back up, a spray of seawater making contact with his face. Flint sighed as Chambers displayed his agitation once more.

"You know why I'm not gonna check it? Because my three sons are meant to be guarding that perimeter with the coastal gun! And I don't want to see that they've broken through his line..." Chambers' face twisted into an unnatural display of gloomy expression. Flint could sense it already before it struck, it was like a deer before it's hunted, knowing what would suddenly come before it actually did. He never saw the missiles coming. But he heard them bursting in from the enemy planes.

BANG!

A mighty explosion rocked the state of the ship, followed by more, creating devastating blows to the lower hull and main deck. Flint watched in horror as Peter Chambers was flung overboard like a ragdoll, screaming and throwing his arms as he plunged headfirst into the lurking waters below, swallowed up by the current. He was followed by the other crew too, menacingly smacking into the ocean. It wasn't long before Flint was thrown over too, but luckily at the last moment, he clung onto the railing. He now was hanging down; he peeked below, imagining the sheer pain of a watery grave.

Helpless.

He heard the swishing of the water below, the feeling of the waves intensely leaping up to drench his back. Fires quickly opened up below the ship, lingering by the stairs, chucking melting sparks into the wind. He tried calling for help, however, under the noise and explosions destroying the ship, he knew it was utterly worthless. His arms were starting to burn. Shoulders giving away by the second. He closed his eyes, accepting his fate. But then, miraculously, he felt an arm tug in his shoulder before he was pulled back onto the ship, dragged a few metres to cover. He saw a face. Hayden Hendrix.

"Hayden! Thank you!" Flint just managed to say before resting his head on the wet floor.

"No worries, but we still need to get out of here!" he replied. It was just at that moment that the huge funnel came cascading down a few metres away from them. The metal clanged and the monstrous noise descended upon him. Hayden was launched sideways into a nearby wall, winded instantly as he slid back down. Flint was crawling towards the centre of the ship when the floor by his hip crumbled way from the impact and fell into the ocean. He scrambled for his life as debris blasted around him, smoke stinging his eyes. All around him, navy airmen and soldiers were bumping into him; running for one of the emergency exit boats one the other side of the ship. Flint heard a deep rumbling sound as he paced himself to some containers just left of the main deck.

SNAP! WHACK!

A wire holding one of the containers in place tore open, scattering rope in all directions. The ship was now turning on its axis encouraging the container to slide down and off into the ocean. The container came barrelling forwards, metal sparks engulfing the terrain. Flint was in the way. And so were others. He leaped to the right side of it, the only one clearing the targeted area. The other men collided into it, screams heard for a deep second. They were killed instantly or rolled with it into the cold-hearted sea. With a face smeared in ash and a body brutally battered, he stumbled to one of the clear stairs painfully, gnashing his soot-covered teeth. He limped there, but his limp became a climb as the boat once again nodded to one side.

BANG! BANG! BANG!

Flint caught sight of one of the airplanes, a German Junkers Ju 88 fighter-bomber, as it became dangerously low to the battleship, unloading whole clips of bombs into the stern. 'Penetrate the hull and you'll take down a whole ship!' was what his father had once told him. It was incredible how his father was still there in his desperate thoughts even when he was on a bombed, sinking ship tipping to one side in the English Channel.

A nearby anti-aircraft station was firing away just yards from Flint, ferociously blasting beams of 5.25-inch bullets at the fighter planes, destroying them mid-air. However, one of the Junkers came whistling down vertically, unloading a whole clip of machine gun bullets into the main body of the weapon. Lead ricocheted off it, bouncing of the tough iron and straight into a soldier loading ammo in beside it, while others sank in, slowly breaking it up. The AA gun had managed to just clip the plane's wing, spinning it in circles and heading straight towards the battleship. The gun suddenly exploded randomly as a stray bullet had whistled into the mainframe wire, triggering a chain of sparks. The navy airman controlling the gun dived to one side but was horrifically caught by the explosion and blown to pieces.

The emergency boats were on the opposite side of the ship, designated near the back hull. Flint had only one option. It was to go below deck and tunnel his way out by the stairs there, it would be much safer and quicker than crossing in open-air surrounded by bombarding German planes. He ran down the melting stairway and into the corridors below, swiftly dodging huge flames and wounded soldiers by the entrance. They were clutching their injuries, slowly being submerged into the rising water helplessly. Flint felt a soaring urge of willingness to reach the rafts, to survive the ordeal. He dashed past the seemingly endless row of bunks set ablaze. Finally, he reached a junction sort of stop, signalling 'bow' or 'stern', he frantically waded down 'stern's' way.

There was much more water here, and it was increasingly rising over his exhausted knees. His knackered arms were dragged along as he waded on. At the end of the corridor, which was around twenty metres more, he detected two soldiers sprinting down the stairs eagerly. One carelessly tumbled into the seeping water; completely covered for a few ticks. His friend knelt down to help him up, but suddenly a wave of flames flew into him from the entrance, totally overrunning him. He awkwardly spun around, like he had been zapped, crying out and slapping himself at the flames, which grew upon him. His body came to an excruciatingly sudden halt. His eyes closed slowly and he dropped into the water. Horrified, Flint leaped past the two, one just lifting himself out the liquid, discovering the other had been burnt to a crisp. Furthermore, he climbed into the open again, the scavenging sun coming out to welcome him in this horrible time, making him squint.

He had come at the right time, or so he thought.

Flint eyed one of the rafts being quickly reeled into the water. To go onto it you had to climb down a singular rope, which was attached to the metal door he had just come out of. It had space for a maximum of ten people, making it quite small. A huge gathering of people were eagerly waiting by the edge of the ship, shoving each other to become the first in line. Some of them were already jumping into the water, which was now around fifteen metres down, to get a head start onto the raft. This was the lowest point on the boat because of the ship now mainly tipping to this side only. Ever since the Titanic thirty-two years ago, all cruise or navy ships had to have enough rafts for the amount of people on board so that all could exit safely; but this was not the case here, half of the emergency boats had been destroyed by the bombs; meaning there wasn't enough for everyone. Thankfully, the raft had been safely deployed onto the water despite all the chaos, bouncing up and down against the trembling waves.

The first man climbed down…only to be met by a shockwave behind that hurled him down into the ocean. A terrified shriek was heard as he belly-flopped in. The current was too strong where he had landed and was sorrowfully sucked into the spinning propellers, blades disintegrating him. That same shockwave had blasted the door of which had the rope tied onto it, making it smack into several soldiers as it tumbled into sea; dragging more men with it. The last dozen remaining dived into the sea, Flint looked down to see small splashes of where they had landed because of how high he was. His mind was having a conflict of itself, wondering whether to jump into the ocean to the raft without a life jacket. *Whatever, there was no time for that!* thought Flint. Obviously, it would be extremely hard to reach the small mode of transport under the pressure of the rolling waves. He decided what he had to do.

Jump.

4 – Impact

Flint felt it as he smacked into the water.

The pain riddled through his body. Mind focusing on swimming back to the surface. The water was freezing, seeping into his boots and creating a very chilly feeling indeed. Air bubbles gurgled out his mouth. He felt his lungs cramp, shoulders completely overworked, aching more by the second. Splashes erupted above him as he continuously swam up, hoping for one thing.

Oxygen.

Finally, his head burst out the water; he took a mighty deep breath, filling his stomach. A sigh of relief swept over Flint's face. He bobbed up and down for a bit, harnessing the energy into his limbs again. He then spotted the raft metres from him. It was severely overloaded with wounded and exhausted soldiers, each begging the officer controlling it to escape from the death zone.

"Just a few men more! They need our help!" the officer bellowed. An atmosphere of rising frustration and anger overtook the scrambling survivors; they helped up the remaining soldiers out of the water, desperate to leave.

"Help!" howled Flint, the energy sapped out of him.

"Come on, quick!" yelled back one of the men, drenched in oil. He stretched out a hand and clung himself to Flint.

"Thank…you!" Flint just managed to say under his breath. Flint clambered onto the raft edge, half his body in the water. He looked up to see Harry Willis, aiding another man's leg, which had broken. Sergeant Brighton was next to the casualty, hoping they would make it through. All the passengers were shivering like crazy, trying to keep themselves warm. A humungous explosion blasted out from the battleship once again, shaking the water violently around it. The ship then began its long descent into the unknown ocean, completely disappearing in minutes, forgotten, collecting algae at the bottom. Flint tapped Brighton on the shoulder,

"You know where we are, sir?"

"Yes, fourteen miles east of Bournemouth. It might take around a day to get there. Hope you're not thirsty," the sergeant replied, relatively calm.

"Actually, I am but okay," Flint replied. "Where's the rest of the squad? I only saw Hayden," asked Flint, curious if anyone had fallen.

"We were all by the rear deck, so luckily we had easy access. The rest of the platoon escaped while they could. James, Hayden and myself stayed behind to operate the AA guns, but that's when Hayden saw you. Private Smith and Lieutenant Cole had some minor burns but nothing much. Like I said, we were first to go," he muttered reassuringly. Flint nodded, distracted by the sun now setting in the eerily quiet distance.

The German Junker bombers had let them be, flying back to France, probably needing fuel or ammunition. He pondered on what they were thinking. Did they know that their squadron of fighters had just slain over three hundred, leaving half that amount stranded in the unforgiving ocean? Of course! They probably were grinning to themselves right now; pleased to report back to their Nazi commanders. Flint closed his eyes rested his head on the edge of the raft, relieved to finally be safe. He dazed to the depths of sleep...

"Wait...watch it!"

Flint dived to cover, his mind muffled and delusional as a mighty black raven swooped by, its bloodshed beak just skimming his foot. Christopher? His brother suddenly had appeared crawling into safety. A vicious squawking sound shrieked out once more, his world spinning as an excruciatingly painful rip tore across his shoulder. The raven was on top of him now, huge black talons clawing into his body as light shimmered around him. The weight was finally supressed by...Hayden? There was a vicious brawl and scramble as the angered raven plunged its beak around his friend's leg, tossing him into the ever-changing day to night sky. Flint was paralysed; all his strength mustered up however it was all the same, nothing changed. It was as if he was there just to spectate it!

"Flint!" barked Hayden as he drifted off into the night sky, hanging in the raven's significant mouth.

Not one muscle could move.

Nothing.

5 – The Home Calling

30 MAY

1944

Flint woke up.

What kind of dream was that!

He realised he was home as the raft swamped against a pit of rocks wrapped in slimy, fresh algae; and waded through the seawater to the dry greenery that lay in front. The terrain in southeast England's coast is usually very rocky in areas; but can be inhabited by a spring of vegetation vital to farmers; a case that came to life in Flint's state. He watched as the waves continuously lapped in by his side, rolling and sprinkling salt, which were dragged back by the sea and plunged back into where it came from. On the beach, dozens of men were resting on the pebbles or preparing a medical tent, which they could also contact rescuers through.

"Mitchell, you all right?" asked Sergeant Brighton generously, his helmet lopsided on his head and sleeves rolled up.

"Yeah, I…I think I'm good." He swallowed after, wiping the stinging water from his eyes.

"Good. Rally on me in five?" Wandering off, he collected the water into his hands and washed the ash off his face and arms.

Flint looked around for Hayden, but there was no immediate sight of him. He was increasingly worried but still believed that Hayden could be in the tent, which had just been set up, even with the sheer amount of voices inside. His feet crunched along the pebbles and he winced every time he used his left leg. He probably had torn a muscle. Flint pulled the clean brown flaps to one side and walked down the tent glancing at each face sitting on the edge. A group were playing with cards, one of them, very wearily, mixing and stacking them up. Others were either sleeping with their heads tucked against the wall of the tent or smoking cigars. The smoke lingered in the air like fog and created a sick putrid sense. He couldn't see Hayden anywhere. Groaning voices were heard outside suddenly, desperate cries of help and medicine, which triggered Flint to limp out into the wind, a beam of sunlight streaking into his detained vision. He reluctantly spotted a figure propped up against a metal rack on the rocks, motionless and aided by the other soldiers. Flint leapt towards them, surprised to see Hayden in a very bad state. There were burns spiralling from both shoulders to his stomach, he had lost one of his shoes and his helmet, there was seaweed entangled across his head. Dried skin was flaking off his cheeks.

"Flint…" he just managed to scarcely moan.

"I'm here and in one piece, so are you thankfully," he muttered as he knelt.

"Private, could we get through?" someone asked rhetorically. He glanced behind him and saw Lieutenant Cole carrying a beige coloured stretcher with Willis. The medic reached into his burnt sachet bag and pulled out a syringe, oozing with medicine, which dripped onto the cracked rocks. He plunged it into Hayden's thigh, a yelp of pain could be heard as he peered at the unexpected needle pinning into his veins. Cole looked down at Flint and told him to get up and help Hayden back to the tent. He nodded and staggered to help him stand up. Shaking and shivering, Hayden tripped over but was caught quickly by Cole, patiently waiting for him to regain his lack of strength. After they had escorted Hayden to the medical area, all the remaining squad members rallied up on Brighton. He was standing commandingly; he did not have his helmet on and was writing final notes on his drawing board next to him. On the board was a detailed map drawing of west France, filled with arrows and various other symbols.

"All right, listen up!" he said, drawing the attention of all the soldiers in his squad. He was just about to speak when Stephens came dashing towards him, clinging his rifle and handing over an A4 sheet of paper; Brighton scowled before shoving the paper back into Stephens' hands, a worried look over his face.

"Anyway, I hope you're all well because I'm not and I do not have time for your personal matters." He stared at Stephens who was fiddling nervously with his sheet before he said what he wanted. "In a week we are about to engage in the biggest invasion this war…and the world, has ever seen. We will be shipped off to Normandy, Sword beach, and then followed up by heading towards the Rhine River." Brighton pointed at several rural and heavily defensive regions on his drawing board.

"All sorts of other units will join us. French, Americans and some Canadians. From there we will push on midland, but we'll focus mainly on the approach for now. After we land, we'll meet again on the eastern Cliffside, where further instructions will lead us northeast towards with the 2nd American Armoured Division and the 9th British RAF corps. Lieutenant Cole?"

Cole nodded and rubbed his short-trimmed beard, he was holding his helmet in his hand and it clanged against his pistol holster. He began to speak under the splashes of the distant calm waters, "Local home guard has finally picked up our radio frequencies we've sent out and reported us to rescue operatives. While they're on their way, we'll be pitched up on the second hill to our left." He pointed steadily at the hill on Flint's right, a green roll of stretching shrubbery and vegetation.

"How long are we going to be up there?" asked Luka Smith, his voice trailing at the end.

"For a while I'm guessing, it's all up to how long the rescuers take. We'll do what we can, don't worry. Any other questions?"

The unit shook their heads stiffly.

"Thank you, Lieutenant Cole," interrupted Brighton, a flash of past and unknown torment swept across his eyes. "Let's go."

The squad exited into different areas, Cruz, Harper and Smith all trudging up the steep, rocky hill whilst Willis wandered singularly to the medical tent tagged along by Stephens. Hayden and Flint joined the other three, wearily using their exhausted limbs to climb up the seemingly forever-going cliff. Flint glanced back to see Brighton and Cole having a growing quarrel, snapping words at each other. He could just make out some muffled words from the top of the cliff.

"You're risking the…" and "Report me then!"

Brighton suddenly stomped off snatching some papers from Cole's hand. The commander turned back and hissed something, but Flint was too far to hear. Cole looked to one side, shaking his head before entering the medical tent. They reached the hill, which they had been ordered, sighing and toppling to the ground, backs resting against the thin strands of grass. In the distance, crops and wheat fields could be seen, gold and light hazel in colour, almost sparkling in the light.

"Lads," Hayden called out. "Imagine having a nice bottle of apple juice freshly squeezed from farms in Devon." This sparked an immediate reaction…and it was definitely not a good one.

"Hayden! What's wrong with you! How am I meant to rest now!" shrieked Cruz, the Spanish accent clearly heard.

"Imagine it though…with ice cubes…" Flint remarked, making the others laugh even more.

"Now that would be something to fight for!" harmonised Jack Harper.

Everyone breathed in deeply, sitting on the hill, sun strobes scattering into their eyes. Flint looked out into the horizon, taking in sights of the cobbled road and freshly cut grass, gleaming in the light. A lone cow could be seen too. Munching in between the shrubs and eager to harvest as much as it could. As well as the mammal, a rusting plough was a few yards away from it, hopelessly sitting their wondering if it would ever get used again. But it wouldn't. Ever since the 20's, manufactured agricultural equipment were hugely developed in urban areas such as India. New machinery was built rapidly across the globe, increasing factory trade and companies.

"Flint, you got any idea what's gonna hit us when we land in France?" asked Hayden, his blistered hand shading his eyes.

"I dunno, hopefully nothing worse than we've experienced already," he steadily replied.

"Hmm, I'm not sure," Hayden grumbled. "I have to admit though it does feel nice being back here."

"Are you mad? I haven't stepped foot on this place for three weeks!" barked Flint. Hayden let out a chuckle, happy that things were finally getting better for the moment. His well-waited for smile was interrupted by a deep and rumbling car engine in the distance, the familiar noise bringing hope to the ones who could hear it.

"Yes!" cried out Luka, bolting upright, his burnt uniform still damp on his back.

"They've come!" Flint also shouted.

A truck appeared across the field, a green basic vehicle that bore a huge red cross sign painted on all sides. It was coming at relatively quick speeds and was chucking dirt and grass into the opposite direction almost like a funnel; chattering beside the wheat. In a matter of moments, it drove up to Flint's boots, stuttering as the engine came to a halt as a tall, slim man took out the keys. The man leapt off the truck and pulled out a metal canister, before banging the roof twice. Out of the back, a squad of medics jumped out, loaded to the max with medical supplies and food. The man then approached Flint who rose up; he brushed the dust of his knees.

"Are you Bravo Six, mate?" asked the soldier. Flint looked at him and pondered. He had never heard of 'Bravo Six'.

"Bravo Six?" the man repeated, rolling his eyes he pulled out a stained slip from his back trouser pocket. "British 3rd Infantry Division?" he added.

"Oh, yes, yes, sir, we are. We also got 8th Company down on the beach." Flint nodded his head towards the sea.

"Good, I'm Corporal Liam, you need anything?" he asked as his hand shook firmly with Flint. Liam felt that Flint's arm was almost like chilling ice, the cold unravelling his skin.

"No."

"Okay, help out these lads over here and set this stuff up on this field." He glanced at the green open space. "Should do."

"Yes, sir."

Flint watched as Corporal Liam wandered off down the rocky slope to the pebbled beach. He kicked up some moss from the ground beneath his foot, the dirt falling back to the earth. Wearily, Flint jogged towards the camo truck and heaved a packeted box of food out, feeling the aching of his arms once more. Flint then placed it on grass and set off for another one. Again, he picked one up and dropped it down.

"Hey! Private? You don't need to do this; get yourself some water. You look like you've just been in a shipwreck," said one of the soldiers. He had a very short moustache and had an ace card popped in his outer rim of his helmet. Flint squinted his eyes and simply nodded slowly while walking over to the water basket. Obviously, they'd never been in combat before.

"I'll hand these out."

"Be my guest," the soldier replied.

The night rolled by, unravelling the stars, which seemed somehow magical in the midst of the dark. Shadows grew up from behind the trees, which slowly darkened the still terrain. All that could be heard was the lapping of the ocean and mutter of the desolate crickets, which had finally settled in the wilderness. Four soldiers parted from the bush line, their faces weary and helmets slanted across their face. Their dark green backpacks overloaded with various objects, which strained their shoulders. One of them spoke in a hushed tone, some strands of his chestnut brown hair falling over his forehead. He had an undoubtedly commanding voice, which left the others heading for the trucks, one stumbled on a small ditch and his comrade pulled him up, asking if he was okay.

"I'm good, thanks," he replied blankly.

"Cole, you drive, you three get in the back," said the commander whilst leaping into the passenger seat. Flint Mitchell, Luka Smith and Hayden Hendrix climbed into the back of the vehicle and sat opposite each other; just managing to see one other through the pitch-blackness. A hurl of engines from other vehicles could be heard behind them, some stuttering before coming to a clean acceleration. Their own engine finally turned on, revealing a dazzle of red and yellow lights, which smothered the darkness. Flint sat up, letting his leg drift out of the back of the van. He felt the machine come to a halt before Cole switched up the gear, enabling the van to move and progress. Dust came barrelling from under and swept with the wind into the distance. He felt like he was just about to drift to sleep when Brighton called out from the front, "We got about three hours ride to the nearest HQ, I suggest you get some sleep now and be ready for the biggest day of your life. We're leaving for Dover at thirteen-hundred tomorrow and then to Sword." He turned back around towards the road and whispered to Cole.

6 – Rough Welcome

It had been nearly a week since the men of the 3rd Infantry Division had been shipwrecked by an unexpected Nazi bombing raid…and they were ready to be shipped off once more to France. They were staying for a few days at Dover's Army Barracks, a relatively calm mood sweeping throughout the period. The Supreme Allied Commander had issued a whole army of blow-up plastic tanks to be sent to Calais as a decoy, which shifted the whole German force. This also resulted in most defensive troops around the border to be reposted further north. However, the Allies were only hours away from launching the riskiest invasion at five beachheads way south, at rural Normandy. These beaches consisted of Juno, Gold, Utah, Sword and Omaha with the overall operation known as 'Overlord'.

There was a mixture of deep feelings across the soldiers. Most anticipated it, not having an idea what they were sailing into; however, the ones who were experienced in any field of the military were absolutely dreading it, including Brighton, knowing they were going to have to single-handedly fight into one of the most brutal conflicts anyone had ever witnessed. Little had come out to Flint about Brighton's past and he was growing more curious by the second. Wondering about what could have happened so horrifically, Flint walked over to his sergeant, who was sketching in his diary contently by an oak table. He had a lit cigar in his mouth, which allowed streams of dark grey smoke to linger around him. Flint approached just as he was about to flick the page and caught him off guard.

"Yes, private," Brighton muttered without looking up. He began to draw a winter fishing port on the blank sheet, which awaited.

"Sir, can I take a seat?" Flint asked nervously with writhing knees.

"Go ahead," he replied intensely. "Just don't be too long. I've got better things to do than waste my time with you…" Nodding and nervous, Flint plucked up the bravery and asked the question which none of his unit had dared ever asked.

"Sir, what happened in your past? Where were you based?"

Brighton stared at him coldly like an icy dagger to the heart.

"You don't need to know, Mitchell," he replied and sighed before adding, "Why? You boys been tellin' stories?"

Flint waited patiently without a reasonable answer, directly looking at the inferior man opposite who was clearly thinking twice about refusing to answer. Brighton rolled his eyes…

"To suit your disrespect? No chance." He sighed until an awkward minute had passed. "What worth is it anyways…it was two years ago, 1942 and—" He rolled his eyes and muttered 'Why am I doing this?' sternly under his breath. He carried on reluctantly despite.

"News had just come past us that Chinese spies had confirmed that Japanese Forces across Burma were too overstretched to penetrate any further west. There were sort of like an elastic band. Pulled to much more in any direction and their entire frontline would collapse. Anyway, back then me and Cole were just privates, part of the mixed British-Indian forces stationed in Assam, India. We had fought earlier that year at the port of Akyab on the Burmese coast, and let me tell you, that ended in complete mayhem and madness. Over five thousand men for not even a blade of grass. Unspeakable. However, after we retreated, some of our platoon was specifically recruited for joining a unit of specially trained men. We were to be placed in very small numbers scattered deep into Japanese-held Burma; this manoeuvre was known as 'Operation Longcloth' and was kept extremely discrete throughout the military. Our organisation was called the 'Chindits' and we even had a special badge that I've kept 'til this day. At first, us two were glad that we weren't going to fight in huge battles no more, but then it struck me…we were heading into the most ferocious and ruthless nation's territory. A kingdom ruled by nothing more than honour, fear and terror. The Japanese Empire. We were all like the men here now, Flint. 'Anticipating the destruction of the axis war machine' as we would chant into the night. But no. It would never be like that. And so in the following month, we were flown under the radar to Burma and dropped with minimal gear into the jungle. The first week wasn't too bad, to be honest. Yes, we did have little food and the merciless jungle against us, but we were not in any 'real' danger as they called it. Plus, we did have each other!"

"Luckily, no Burmese natives had snitched us out. And if they said they were, like that couple of tourists from Istanbul, we were sure that they'd been taken care off. After a while, I guess, of collecting various intel sources and laying mines on military train tracks, those Japs got curious. They started sending a couple in at a time into the jungle. And trust me, we made sure they couldn't escape nor tell what was happening. But after we destroyed their underground power station, they came flooding in, hundreds of them, searching under every rock and behind every tree. We then lost radio contact with our other Chindit squads further south and we feared for the worst. Our unit had heard about the brutal P.O.W camps in the east, where torture and suicide was a daily occurrence. It would probably be better off if they were dead. None of us fancied to live caged up and beaten for the rest of our lives. But one night however, we made a small campfire in a ditch to hide its light from any onlookers. Cole was sleeping with the others in tents while me and this other soldier, I think it was Richardson, was keeping guard around the perimeter; our ears alerting us to whatever so much made a creak. I had an M1 Thompson in hand and a machete strapped across my leg. So I did definitely feel relatively safe against Japanese Arisaka rifles and pistols. I mean, we were 'special forces' so each one of us had a field telephone and more advanced equipment. We were at watch post for around an hour when I heard a slice and a deep gurgle. I wanted it to be Richardson maybe hitting a low hanging branch or something, but it was nothing even near that. At all.

"I investigated what the noise was, my heart racing at every step I managed to take. Then I saw it. Richardson was sprawled on the floor. Dark blood was seeping out from his throat and he lay completely lifeless. I called out for the other Chindits when suddenly this one screaming Jap ran at me from under the cover of darkness and shoved his bayonet straight through the edge of my neck."

Sergeant Brighton pulled down his collar and revealed the hideous scar dragging across the length of his pale neck. Flint was surprised he was telling the history so dramatically; it probably had struck a lost chord inside. The sergeant spat on the floor in a hateful manner and continued.

"Of course, I tumbled to the jungle floor with him, his face was so desperate to try and get me over and done with quickly, that he even gave me an extra boost to be first to it! His Japanese uniform was extremely camouflaged with grass and weeds poking out of every corner. No wonder poor old Richardson couldn't see him coming. For a few seconds, there was a tug of war between the rifle, I pleaded with him, urging him not to shoot. He shot. Since the bayonet was already through my neck and stuck there, the bullet tore through the rest and leapt into the looming forest behind. My ears rang and my whole body filled with soaring pain as he brought out his own personal dagger. It had a few words of Japanese carved across the white handle…probably some ancient warrior stuff. He hissed loudly before lowering the knife onto my forehead. It pinched my skin, getting deeper by the second. Just before he could swing sideways; his whole body flung backwards, a cloud of blood spraying into my face. I saw Cole sprint towards me, frightened of the injury I had just sustained.

"The Japanese soldier was in a mighty tension of pain, desperately trying to crawl away as blood leaked from his chest; his aim to disappear into the dark jungle. Our squad leader, Chamberlain, strolled towards him and snatched a handgun from his holster and pointed it square at his head. He fired the gun twice…ending the young man's life. We thought that was all and were positive so. With the help of a stretcher, I returned back to camp with the medic, Jonathan McInkton who patched me up inside the medical tent. Chamberlain radioed in towards HQ however, no reply was heard. Someone had jammed the system and broken the connection wires…

"Suddenly, we were bombed by an armoured train a few miles away. Huge pockets of earth cascaded up around us taking Chamberlain and a few others with it, leaving only seven of the original twelve left. To make matters worse, we were ambushed by a squad of more Japanese, bullets whizzing past our heads as we scattered into the jungle. They hit Kabir, the local Indian escort, through the throat, Mac several times in the chest and my friend from primary school, Toby, in the head twice. I don't know what happened to the rest, though. Probably dead as well by the most chance. I limped more into the jungle, managing to shoot some of them with my Thompson before crashing down a hill.

"I lay there for what seemed an eternity, Flint. I couldn't get up because my whole body lay paralysed, pain ringing through my brain. I must've been on the bottom of that muddy mound for at least two days before rescue managed to arrive. Turns out that it had been only me and Cole who had managed to escape from the ordeal. Coincidence? No. We were just good friends. When I got back, all the other Chindit groups that were left rapidly withdrew and the whole

'Operation Longcloth' was a bust. No British nor Indian soldier has stepped foot on Burmese soil since that day…"

7 – Blood on the Sand

"You are about to embark upon the Great Crusade, toward which we have striven these many months. The eyes of the world are upon you. The hopes and prayers of liberty-loving people everywhere march with you. You will bring destruction of the German war machine, the elimination of Nazi tyranny over the oppressed peoples of Europe, and for security for ourselves in a free world. Your task will not be an easy one. Your enemy is well trained, well equipped and battle hardened. He will fight savagely. I have full confidence in your courage and devotion to duty and skill in battle.
We will accept nothing more than full victory!"

The main allied battleship for Sword beach heaved itself across the English Channel, navy sailors working tirelessly to keep the beast of a boat afloat as they listened to General Dwight Eisenhower power on with the speech. The *HMS Warspite* was packed to the brink with grey metallic landing crafts, which were carried on the underside of the immense hull. On the other hand, some were deployed from other surrounding ships such as the American *USS Nevada* and *HMS Nelson*. Flint however, was sailing with the *HMS Warspite,* bouncing on the endless lines of waves that buried itself into the battleship. He heard the roar of the naval guns as they boomed towards the French land opposite them, smashing into the cliffs and shattering machine gun bunkers. The early, overcast morning sky lay blanketed in buzzing allied bombers over the shoreline, fighter pilots slicing through the dense clouds and even a prowling huddle of huge zeppelins. A deafening screech was created as the battleship pivoted right, heading towards the rumbling mainland. Himself? He didn't know how to describe it. But the raw feeling of excitement and dread combusted into each other. Flint climbed down the rear ladder and walked around the immaculate ship towards where the landing crafts would soon be deployed.

"Bravo Six on me!" shouted Sergeant Brighton, his voice echoing through the tunnel.

"Come on! We got fifteen minutes 'til the invasion starts! Let's move!" commanded Cole.

The whole squad rushed single-filed down the stairs to the dispatch zone, Harry Willis lead and threw the climbing rig down the side of the ship. It splashed in the ice-cold water below and hooked onto the first landing craft.

"Load up!" Brighton ordered.

Stephen O'Leary was clumsy on his feet and shaking tremendously, his hands swaying wildly as he tried to catch the edge of the swinging rig. Just before he climbed down, Brighton grabbed him by his shoulder and took him aside. The sea salt came spraying over board, smacking into the platoons helmets and backpacks. Flint watched onwards as Brighton shouted words of motivation into the young second lieutenant's ear, trying to make himself clear under the ferocious roar of the boats and planes. Flint's fingers clutched the M1 Garand nervously and felt the cold, deadly weapon in his hands. Fixing the helmet across his head, Flint grasped hold of the wet rig. Hayden followed him from behind also incredibly anxious and holding his own M1 Garand. Flint began to descend down the rig when suddenly a wave hit the landing craft below head on. He hung on as the water wildly vibrated the ropes. He hoped it wouldn't make him unexpectedly fall in.

"You all right there?" Hayden asked loudly from above. Flint nodded gently, squinting as he looked up, salt stinging his eyes once again. Flint managed to jump down into the small boat, which was now carrying around fifteen people. He could just make out Ruben Cruz at the front with Jack Harper who were talking to each other uncomfortably. Hayden and finally Brighton entered the landing craft behind and signalled the driver, who was looking extremely frightened, to go. The driver closed his eyes for a split-second and turned the wheel right towards the beach.

"Mitchell! You good to go?" Brighton asked from behind him.

"Yes, Sergeant, I'm just thinking," Flint's reply was quick.

A trembling minute passed.

"At least we're not based at Omaha," asked Brighton out of the blue trying to calm his men down.

Jack commented with a deep sigh as he clutched his helmet, "Tell me about it. Apparently they couldn't even get out the water and the bombs hit 'em."

The drumming continued. Silence spread between the men.

"We're still the first division onto the beach, though!" Hayden let out in the looming silence.

"Well." Lieutenant Cole paused. He wiped the sweat and seawater from his forehead. "It's just gonna have to be the sacrifice we've gotta make."

They shook as the boat started to speed across the sea, waves galloping and encircling all around them. The whole squad looked towards Sword beach directly in front. It was a mess of black, suffocating smoke and ash that slowly rose towards the looming clouds. The cliffs were astonishingly huge and drastically towered the black ocean, rocks cascaded down from above and cracked against the coral, splitting into multiple directions. Flint felt incredibly insignificant and had the deep feeling he was being held down by an iron fist. Numerous fires, which burnt like infernos, spread across the coastline and illuminated the chaotic surroundings even more.

"Focus in, Bravo Six, we're nearly there," ordered Brighton as he stacked loaded magazines of ammo into his polished belt.

"It's gonna be kind of hard to do that with a beach full of machine guns a few miles away," muttered Hayden. A few of the other soldiers let out a chuckle; however, others were beginning to understand the dark side of it…

"Just stick to the mission, it will see you through," added Brighton.

"I'll do my best…" muttered Flint worryingly.

Flint glanced, with an eye of burning salt, towards his right flank at the distant Juno beach, a vast array of tiny Canadian boats landing onto the sand. Drumming gunfire could be heard from the beach…horrendous scatters of explosions and grenades. Most infantry shots were muffled by the screaming of men and the frantic bombings of the planes overhead. There were dozens of landing crafts around just like them, all packed to the brink with petrified young men. Some experiencing their last seconds…

"Twenty seconds!"

The sand of the beach came ever closer and the water ever lighter. It was just now in those final moments that Flint spotted Cole to his right, muttering motionlessly to his own Chindits badge. It seemed as if he still hadn't forgotten the nightmares that had scarred him in Burma, just like Brighton. Flint felt the booming of the bombs shuddering in his chest and twisting his heart. Bullets flashed past the boat from heavily defended machine gun bunkers from the cliffs. The squad began screaming as the reality of what was about to happen struck them. There were barbed wire and Czech hedgehogs (X-shaped iron objects) littering the beach, menacingly looking at the landing crafts edging nearer by the second. All the backpacked soldiers in the landing craft were hunched forward, prepared to rush up as the seawater came splashing overboard into their faces. Suddenly, the boat next to them was annihilated into a furious explosion of great shades of scarlet and jet-black. Shards of steel and iron scattered in all directions; one single soldier's leg flew up lifeless with it. The heat from the blast radiated against Flint's cheek, burning his skin immensely. Suddenly, the landing craft slammed back and he was thrown forward into Lieutenant Cole. The driver glanced up from his wheel and screamed hopelessly.

"It's stuck—!"

A bullet zipped through his forehead and he tumbled out the boat.

SPLASH!

The next thing he knew, a mighty thud vibrated through the bullet-holed landing craft and Brighton wailed something he never wanted to hear.

"Ramp down!"

Like a hammer, the metal wall dropped onto the sand and revealed a whole platoon of inexperienced, petrified young men.

"Go! Go! Go!" shrieked Brighton.

ZING! SMACK!

Instantly, as Cruz was at the front, a hoard of bullets zipped into his body and viciously threw him down.

RATATATATA!

More bullets sprayed into the landing craft, blood splattering all over Flint as he tried to dash forward, adrenaline pumping under the shreds of meat. Men around him fell to the floor, riddled with metal as they crumpled onto the deck with guts spilling out. Flint watched from the back as half his platoon was gunned down on top of each other, blood spraying into their faces or over the sides. Bodies slumped onto each other more by the second only a few minutes after breathing and smiling in the light of dawn. He had to move or he would be next.

Brighton, Harper and Hayden launched themselves over the sides; desperately dodging the killer fragments. Flint tripped over a lone arm and tumbled towards the entrance of the boat, whistling bullets ricocheting all around him. The loud pierce of the lead hitting the sides created long twang sounds, which rang wildly in Flint's ear. Frantically scrambling over dead bodies, another squad on his right deployed onto the beach. In half an instant, half of them came collapsing onto the sand smothered in melting fire. Their cries were heard distinctively as they were gunned down without mercy into the water.

Flint bolted forward off the landing craft and plunged into the knee-deep water, feeling the icy ripples shatter around his limbs. Bullets chucked up liquid, blue or red, all around him, the whining sounds filling him with terror and monstrosity. Somehow, he managed to stumble away from the boat and towards the beach. He looked for the nearest iron hedgehog to hide behind. The bitter cold of the sea and wind rushed up against him. He clawed his teeth together and kept going, muttering words to himself.

"Incoming!"

BOOM!

A huge artillery bomb cascaded into the water a few metres from him and the noise felt like it had destroyed his eardrums. He clung on to his wet yet burnt helmet and rifle as Jack Harper staggered his way towards him. They waded together out the water and onto the dry land, the sand sticking on them as they staggered on.

RATATATATA!

Almost a dozen bullets burrowed into Harper, his blood came squirting out, spilling onto the sand. He awkwardly spun to the floor, utterly shocked that he had been hit without mercy.

"Flint, help…me!" he pleaded slowly, half his face covered in wet sand.

"Okay! Just com—" Almost a whole clip of MG42 bullets whizzed over Flint, sending him ducking against the rusty metal. "Quickly! Just come quickly!"

He crawled his way desperately to Flint who had his hand outstretched, but suddenly, a whistling bullet hit through the cheek. Harper's helmet flew off as his head dug into the sand.

"No!" screamed Flint aggressively.

He hesitated, horrified for a moment, then rose up incredibly quickly and bolted for the next hedgehog, feeling the heat as the bullets just skimmed him. All around him, soldiers threw themselves for cover while constantly dodging enemy fire. They were all tightly packed together, using one another as meat shields.

"We gotta keep moving! Do not group up!"

A medic limped past Flint, his medicine bottle and bandages already out as he made his towards a handless officer. More enemy barrages battered the coastline as the infantry divisions steadily made progress along the beach. Explosions, deep and angry, rocked the very earth around Flint almost taking him off his feet. He glanced to his right and was met with the sight of screaming, crawling soldiers, trying to disappear behind the barbed wire. The same medic was now aiding the injured casualty, fiddling with his torn hand. A mushroom of red exploded from the top of the medic's helmet and he fell slowly to one side, motionless, arms outstretched. The sand rubbed down Flint's neck and was inside his uniform and ripped boots.

BANG! WHACK!

A small fragment of an artillery shell, which exploded a few feet away, caught Flint's shoulder, wedging itself between the flesh. He shrieked astonishingly loudly for a medic and one came hurtling towards him with a look of shock upon him. Pain rushed through his body like the bullets flying past, getting worse by the second. The men around him were launched off their feet or hammered into the ground by the sheer atrocity of the enemy. Sand flicked up all around and the constant snapping sound enraged the battlefield.

"Thank you…thank you…" Flint just managed to whisper as the medic by him stabbed a syringe into his upper arm. A wince of pain stretched across his face, wondering if the next pain he would indulge would be a bullet in the back. Surprisingly, the drained medic pulled out a pair of tweezers and before Flint could say anything, yanked at the irregular piece of shrapnel.

"You're gonna be okay, pal!"

"Arghhh!" Flint yelped in pain.

After the medic had finished, he swung his M1 Garand across his back and clutched at his bleeding wound while still hiding behind the hedgehogs where he decided was safe. Or so he thought. A whistling shell came lobbing over from the bunkers and erupted near Flint, sending himself and the medic flying metres in the air. He crashed down with a huge thump and immediately started crawling again despite his minor injuries. His body was in that state of pure survival mechanisms, where nothing is processed, yet all is taken in for the greater good of the human. Shaken, he rose up and sprinted for a small crater just ahead of him near some blown barbed wire, multiple strands of sweat and seawater ran down his forehead. British soldiers all around him were bundled together behind all sorts of cover, from miniature ditches to dead bodies, but the unlucky ones were still dazed in a bloody, empty space, machine gunned down onto the sand horrendously. Spread across the beaches sand lay random body bits, which sat leaking with blood. It was a truly unforgettable sight.

A chatter of MP40 fire burst past Flint and rained down into the man behind savagely. Shrieks were let out. The smoke and ash clogged the back of his throat and tasted of cordite, which choked him. Finally, he managed to leap down into the crater, joined by other comrades. As he had his back to the machine gun bunkers, he witnessed the mayhem and destruction. Never had they experienced such pain and anguish. A landing craft had been hit on its underside. The boat slowly tipped over into the grey ocean waters. Flames engulfed the whole group of men as they leaped out the sinking craft, drowning in the deep murky waters.

One slim, singular teenager heaved a bullet-ridden Bangalore just behind some scatters of barbed wire, nervously edging his way forwards under the gunfire.

"Come here! Now!" Flint called out to the soldier, cupping his hands over his mouth. The young man signalled worryingly back, stating that he was on his way. Hayden fell just beside Flint into the steep ditch, sand covering his face and hair. He spat onto the floor, blood coming with it.

"You all right?" shrieked Flint. Hayden looked mentally battered and nodded slowly to him. The teenager arrived in the hole and was exhausted too. He had a strong cockney accent yet still sounded increasingly vulnerable.

"So much for this beach to be a peaceful one!"

Biting his lip, Flint spoke in a focused tone of voice. "Look! I'm gonna take the Bangalore and – watch it!" he shrieked. Another huge shell blasted extremely close to the trio. Flint heard muffled screams after it went off and peeked over the lip of the crater. The medic who had treated him was now squirming on the floor, his face in a distorted look of pain. Flint didn't realise what was wrong until he was dragged to cover by a nearby soldier. Blood was flooding out from where his leg was meant to be.

CRACK!

A sniper bullet blasted into Flint's helmets and it flew off out of the ditch, rolling in a circle before falling down into the crater again. The impact nearly shattered his skull, but he forced himself to drastically calm down. He panted rapidly.

"Flint! I'll take this forward! Cover me!" Hayden ordered as he snatched the Bangalore from the kid. He pulled himself over the crater and sprinted towards the line of barbed wire, the bomb rocking in his hand. A whole squad of new soldiers entered the shell crater, some brutally injured.

"Go!" roared the teenager who then clenched his helmet and stormed over. The whole unit obeyed and screamed as they charged forward, constantly trying to dodge the infinite bullets that whistled their way towards them. Flint hip-fired at the bunkers, distracting them as he streaked on, feeling the cold recoil of the weapon as it fired in his hands.

"Take cover!" alerted one running.

A huge wave of artillery bombs cascaded towards them.

BANG!

A deafening noise erupted as multiple explosives detonated along the beach-line. Flint was thrown off his feet, bewildered by the impact. His mind raced, savaged by the adrenaline and fear as staggered back up and raced through the smoke once more. Everything was barely visible.

"Keep moving forward!"

Yet as he trudged onwards, he passed more rows and rows of bodies and bits of bodies scattered along the sand. Finally, he spotted Hayden and helped him prepare the Bangalore torpedo whom was shaking too violently to operate it.

"Get out the way!" warned Flint as he shoved the long pole into the barbed wire. Almost at once, Hayden covered his head with the other soldiers, waiting impatiently for it to blow.

"Fire in the hole!" bellowed Flint as he tore at the detonator.

8 – Loss and Liberty

A mighty explosion erupted and now that the barbed wire had been blasted apart, they were off the sandy part of the beach and onto the grass smothered in dew. The opening allowed the weary soldiers to charge once again through it, more men collapsing to the floor. Flint was the last to go and watched as his comrades around him were shot wildly, colliding down and entangling themselves with the shrubs. Because they were so close to the bunkers now, the Germans were starting to hurl hand-grenades down into them. The blast radius was short however, the shrapnel came bursting out between the nearby soldiers; forcing them painfully to the ground without multiple limbs. Around thirty more men joined them as they raged onto Bunker Delta, as it had been called. The battalion finally made it to the bunker's walls, resting their exhausting backs on the vines that rooted upwards. *Finally! We're out the firing line!* thought Flint. Brighton suddenly came dashing over to lead, covering his head from the machine gunner that was a few metres away inside.

"Follow me!" he commanded.

Sergeant Brighton continued over some dusty outside steps and led his men to the main entrance of the bunker, ordering them to prepare their weapons. The gunner could be heard from the inside, blasting away at his pocket position, which granted perfect cover. They all filed up against the wall, leaning on it to restore energy. Hayden and the sergeant were on the left side of the door while Flint was with the others on the opposite.

"We got a flamethrower?" asked Brighton.

Stephens, who now had come up the steps to the iron bunker door, nodded his head quickly. Flint had noticed that his helmet had gone and his head revealed a deep cut, which rounded from his left ear to the middle of his head. The flametrooper ascended from up the other side of the bunker and reported to Brighton. He had the uniform and helmet of a normal soldier, dark green and basic, however he had two large grey cylinders strapped on his back and a long, tangled tube, which attached to his M2 flamethrower. He looked burnt, which was ironic, and deeply concerned about what he was walking into.

"I'll open this and then do your work." He pointed at the large metal door, which lay in front of him. Brighton smirked slightly and then kicked the door wide open, revealing around five men in German uniforms who were each hunched over their own MG42. One, who was loading another 250-bullet clip, glanced back to see a British flametrooper filling the doorway with his broad shoulders, a sickened expression swept across his face.

"*Bitte! Bitte! Nein!*" the German cried.

The flametrooper only now saw that the soldier was around fifteen, but he didn't care, they were German. Whoever fights for Germany, dies for Germany. The German army needed all they could get as they were slowly slipping in service men. Upon hearing the cry, the other guards pivoted around empty handed and were met with an inferno-like blaze of heat, hurling them against the walls and melting them where they stood. Their screaming lasted for a short while until it faintly died down, which gave a sigh of relief to the squad outside. It was too much. The flametrooper stepped back out into the light, a large shell-like silhouette behind him. He grinned mildly at the mayhem he had just ignited before scowling to himself and trudging to Brighton. Flint looked to his left and spotted three more bunkers stacked on the side of the rocky sloping hill, each with huge strands of machine gun fire exiting them.

"All right, listen up, Alpha Company wants us to push further North to the remaining bunkers. We'll have to cut through the backline trenches to make it there swiftly so that the rest of our boys on the beach are safe. Let's go!" Sergeant Brighton ordered. He led and aimed his M1 Garand while running at the other bunkers in case of snipers. The trenches were dug behind the bunkers and were neatly ordered in winding lines, which stretched approximately fifty metres. They were mainly quite muddy and slippery however it was not too bad around this area, only further back were the real mud-lands. Their platoon zigzagged through the trenches, still hearing the mighty bangs and drumming across the beach. A stray bullet suddenly whizzed over Flint's head, cracking into to a damp sandbag just feet way.

"Get down!" snapped Stephens.

Flint crouched across the rotting fence of the trench and peeked over to see two German soldiers aiming at his squad. One, who had a white scarf whipped around his neck, loaded a fresh magazine of ammo into his MP40 while the other was struggling nervously to unjam his rifle.

"Sergeant! Two hostiles ten o'clock!" whispered Flint.

"I see them. Flint, Stephens, and Smith, flank right while me and Johnson will whip left. Take the bunker when you can!" ordered Brighton in a hushed tone.

Stephens led first eagerly trying to impress his commander. Flint followed him as they descended into the deep end of the trenches, twisting and turning routes while still listening to the cries and shatters on the beach.

"Come on! We gotta help 'em!" Stephens announced with shaking passion.

They trod a few steps before vile disaster struck…unfortunately, because Stephens was so focussed on taking on the bunker a few metres away, he didn't spot the lurking, dangling wire which stretched thinly and elegantly across the width of the trench. The two capsules, which the wire was attached to, were smartly hidden behind some crates of broken beer bottles and burnt cigars.

BOOM!

"Arghhh!" Stephens yelped as he was blasted into the side of the trench.

The explosion threw Flint and Smith, who was close behind, back and dazed them horrendously. Smoke rose up and hung in the air. Flint's senses were drained and visibility low. It took a while to recover, but when he did, he lifted himself off the ash-blanketed ground and stumbled towards the tripwire bomb casualty. Luckily, Stephens was unconscious; however, there was significant bleeding from his left thigh and his shoulder. Flint swiftly snatched his medical pack from off his chest and tried to open it, the dark green sachet covered in red. He was shaking intensely, which made him spill all the medical contents onto the muddy floor. Luka Smith then finally trudged his way over to Flint, a sour look on his face. He muttered a few words at the motionless body of Stephens, whose mouth still gulped for oxygen.

"Smith, help me!" Flint urged, trying to collect all the wet bandages. He then added, "Apply these, I'm gonna get a medic!"

Luka crouched down by the victim and nodded silently as if in a trance. Flint took his M1 Garand off his back and climbed over the fence carefully minding the shards of glass, which were now rooted into the edges. He jumped over the barbed wire and towards the grey bullet-ridden bunker. Johnson, the flametrooper, and Brighton had made their way to the entrance once again about to breach and in position. The big push across the beach had finally erupted and over a hundred of men came storming over the short hill and into the trenches. Suddenly, as they came, a whole division of enemy soldiers came rushing into the dugouts too, machine guns already prepared and mounted into the mud. Brighton breached into the bunker, rapidly shooting the Germans who tried to sprint out. Johnson then lighted them up as they tried to bayonet charge into the British soldiers who had just arrived. Some actually managed to do so and plunged their blades deep into the allied chests; forcing them onto the ground in screaming, agonising pain. Out of nowhere, a whole new Nazi platoon burst from their right coming straight up to the Brit's faces. Hand-to-hand combat had erupted just outside the second bunker.

A German struck into the man next to Flint, head-locking and slamming him onto the dirt. Flint, clambering back up bruised and distorted, pulled out his M1 Garand to shoot; however, another German tackled him to the floor, dislodging him of his weapon and slamming his fist into Flint's face. He then grabbed the weapon and aimed it steadily towards the head, a cold, killer look in his eyes. He was just about to pull the trigger when Brighton came from behind and smacked him in the back of his head with a nearby shovel. A crack sound echoed as the German fell to one side and lay still on the ground, blood beginning to leak from underneath his grey helmet. Brighton winked and continued to batter more incoming axis soldiers, smashing his weapon into their ribs and briskly finishing them off. Flint had never experienced such dark hatred towards another human being than what the others near him were showing. All around him, men were using any melee weapon they could find. Whether it be a slamming plank or a lashing string of barbed wire. All to survive. Another German came fiercely bayonet charging towards Flint, sweat dripping onto his cloak and badge labelled 'Hans'. Flint narrowly dodged and pounded his right fist into Hans' back, which crippled him to the floor. He was bending over winded and when he glanced around, he was met with the cold hard feeling of a fist to his cheek. Flint was suddenly shoved from behind onto the German, who was now screaming wildly, "*Hilfe! Hilfe!*"

Tangled in a mess of mud and debris, Hans tried one last-ditch effort and reached for his Luger from under his grey-buttoned cloak. Flint saw the object come out from under the jacket and quickly scrambled to take off his helmet so that he could use it as a weapon.

BANG!

The gunshot rang out between all the other noises and luckily, the bullet ricocheted off Flint's helmet that he was covering over his face, the piece of lead darting into the smoke covered sky. Flint swung the helmet with all his might continuously into Han's face, knowing he would deeply regret on what he was doing. He decided to stop after four hits, realising there was now a whole pool of blood encircling him and the victim. He stared at the pale bloodied face, knowing that he had just ended a young man's life, fighting for a cause that he wanted to be nothing part of. Wiping his blood-stained hands onto his jacket, he took out his carved knife from behind his heel in case of another lethal attack.

More than two hundred men were engaged in the melee combat, each one British or German, fighting for their lives in the pain stake. And it wasn't over yet. A whole fresh batch of young Brits who had just taken out the third bunker came barrelling towards the scene. Each armed with a Lee-Enfield; they helped greatly as they picked lone Germans off one by one.

Brighton hollered, "Come on! They're on the back foot! They've got a few left, lads!" as he thumped an assault trooper into some nearby ammo crates.

A British officer stood cautiously between the whole battle, pinpointing the last Germans one by one with his Browning 9mm as they came scavenging towards him. Suddenly, a thudding sound was heard and when Flint turned around, he witnessed the officer brutally fumbled to the ground by a pair each giving revenge on what he had done. He then realised it was the same pair who guarded the entrance of the bunker earlier. The white scarf and nervous teenager. They were the last two German survivors left. Flint bolted towards them with his knife, clenching hard on it as he shoved the blade into the teenager's lower stomach. He let it slide in, blood pouring out. Perplexed and almost frozen-like, the German dropped to the ground, the knife sticking out.

"*Sohn! Meine kinder! Du hast meinen Sohn getotet...*" the white scarfed man mumbled heartbrokenly.

A solemn tear rolled down his cheek, showing how weak and frail he was now and deep the effect of what Flint had done. The German levelled down and knelt beside the dead corpse, his face hid away, crying. Flint then realised. He had killed his son. A twist of sorrow erupted across him, frightened that he could call himself a murderer. He gulped slowly. Even with all the chaos and mayhem, nothing bothered Flint and the German as they both felt the pain and downcast swallow the air around them.

"Listen…" Flint brought himself up to apologise painfully.

He had to say something. He felt the force of dark misery sweep over him as he tried, but the words wouldn't come out. The father looked up to Flint who was standing over him, his face smothered in blood and agony. He slowly raised his hands up, surrendering. His lips began to move.

BANG!

The father shuddered.

Horrified, he looked down at his chest; a dark red seeping hole opened up and began to slowly engulf into the rest of his muddy uniform. He fell beside his son. Eyes wide open, staring into the sky. The one place where it is peaceful. Brighton slotted his handgun into his holster. The gun having one less bullet. He wasn't even slightly moved about the action of killing a surrendering, devastated dad.

"You ain't no murderer. This is war," the sergeant muttered before he helped the crawling officer back to his feet. The fifty-year-old quietly thanked both of them and limped to the bunker, seeking cover and water.

"Check their bodies, men!" a cry could be heard. Flint remembered to get back to Smith and Stephens for a medic, but there weren't any left except for Harry, who was trying to take his knife out of a soldier. He looked traumatised and definitely stuck out between the other men with his bright red cross helmet and blood stained armband.

"Harry! Stephens is hit!"

"Bring him, I got my stuff here."

Flint dashed along the line of trenches, frequently having to leap over an injured allied soldier or dead German. He saw Smith aiding Stephens with…Hayden! Hayden was now applying pressure to the wounds and his face lit up as soon he spotted Flint running towards him. He caught his breath and exclaimed, "Flint!"

"Hayden, are you all right?" he asked sternly.

"I'm good, I think," Hayden said, checking his burnt elbows.

"How's Stephens doing?"

"Well, from what I can see, broken collarbone, fractured elbow, two very deep cuts along his left arm and another dozen between his thigh and foot. Got proper done there he did," Smith responded instantly.

"How did we not see that tripwire!" Flint's rage built up and exploded.

"Flint, the thing's practically invisible! You need to have some good eyes to see that string two centimetres off the ground," Hayden replied, trying to calm his friend down.

Flint peered at Hayden, trying to process the 'pathetic excuse' he had just received, and slammed the bandages into the soggy mud.

"I've had enough of all of this! All this carnage!"

He shrieked and attacked Hayden, a violent tussle as they rolled around on the floor slopping in mud and strain.

"Stop! Stop!"

It was Luka who raised his voice, grabbing Flint by the backpack as he wildly swung a punch, flinging him to the trench wall and keeping his arm around his neck. Flint gurgled for air as he slowly came back to his natural thoughts.

"You're not the only one here, Flint! We're in here now, we're not gettin' out! We jus—" Luka strengthened his grip around Flint's neck as he tried to desperately squirm free. "...Have to keep going!"

Luka released his arm and watched as Flint crawled across in the sludge, gasping for precious mouthfuls of air. Hayden rubbed his chin, minor bruising appearing and lifted himself up whilst speaking.

"Okay, forget it, we don't have the equipment to fix Stephens so let's get him to Harry. He's just by the bunker. He'll help." It wasn't an invitation; it was a command. Flint looked in the opposite direction as he lifted Stephens carefully onto his shoulders.

"On me!"

He climbed once again over the trench onto the wet grass, galloping down towards the bunker.

"Smith! Keep guard in front!" Hayden announced as he realised that the other two were vulnerable to a surprise attack.

"Got it!" Smith came bursting in front, slowly moving forward with Flint.

"You want me to carry him?" asked Smith, seeing the strain across Flint's bruised neck.

"Nah, I'm...I'm good. How about you keep going?"

"Sure thing," he replied bluntly. Flint looked at the dark ocean ahead as the waves kept coming in with the landing crafts, the sun still not reaching noon yet. They looked like small black dots in the horizon, which floated calmly towards them, eager to land upon foreign shore. However, looking at all the bodies littering the beach and the smoke and fires illuminating them, he would've never wanted to come here in a million years.

Trudging over another young, battered German body, Flint spotted Harry by the bunker aiding another man's throat. The units medic was wearing no helmet and had his green, long-sleeved overalls pulled up to his elbows, as if trying not to stain them anymore as they were!

Just when Flint was about to call for him, a man popped up from some broken shrubs and pointed his MG42.

"*Treten Sie zuruck! Komm zuruck!*" he shrieked in various German commands. Nearly all the men in the location heard the rant and lazily scrambled for their rifles, all of which were stacked untidily against the walls of the trenches. Surprised and in dead stalemate, Flint slowly dropped Stephens onto the grass, raised his hands and signalled the others to do so as well.

"Hey! I said don't move, you fool!" the abductor ordered in German and gazed with lenses of hatred at Flint's eyes. "Pick him back up!"

Flint noticed the saying and slowly heaved Stephens, with a groan, back up over his shoulders. The German suddenly abandoned his LMG and rapidly snatched out his Luger pistol from his back pocket.

"No! Wait!" Smith screamed as the German yanked him to the side and pointed the gun at side of the lone British soldier's head.

"Stop!" screamed Hayden, still watching nervously as the German tightened his grip on the trigger, which was millimetres from Luka Smith's face.

"Flint…" spluttered Smith as he urged for help. Flint, disobeying the attacker's orders, neatly laid Stephens on the ground while trying to communicate to his enemy, persuading him to let Smith go.

"Let…me…outta zere…" whispered the German quietly to Flint.

"Okay, don't worry we will. But only if you do the same to him," replied Flint calmly, nodding at Smith who began to squirm away from the pistol pointed at his head.

"No!"

"Hey…hey calm down!" Flint shouted, clearly distressed. "Don't make me give you a countdown!"

"No!"

Flint shook his head and watched as Smith started sweating wildly, water dripping down onto his neck and trickling onto the wobbling hand of the German. He looked distraught and not fit to die. Not yet.

"*Heil Hitler!*" screamed the German. He let the gun go off in his hand, a single bullet rocketing into Smith's head, collapsing him to the floor. However, for the Nazi, he was shot from nearly every possible angle and was almost dancing as he was riddled with bullets. Flint froze as both bodies dropped. Mixed emotions swept in as he contemplated on what just happened. A British rifleman walked over to Smith's body as it lay on the grass after booting the German's – he checked his pulse and signalled the obvious news to Flint.

"Bravo Six rally on me!" Brighton announced as he steadily made his way towards the bunker. Flint picked up Stephens once more and brought him to the bunker, calling out for Harry. Laying the second lieutenant on a large, rectangular oak table, Flint reapplied the damp bandages on and investigated the infected injuries. Harry paced in, throwing a broken syringe onto the floor, and glanced at Stephens' leg before he unzipped his medical pack.

"What's happened?"

Flint explained while Harry studied his shoulder, constantly feeling if blood was still leaking out.

"Looks as if it's all right for now. However, his calf is bleeding badly from the cut on his thigh. Gonna be tough one to strap up, but I'll take it from here."

Flint and Hayden nodded anxiously and scurried at the room as Harry revealed a long pair of stainless-steel scissors.

"He'll be all right, you think?" said Flint with a hint of worry.

"It depends on his infection, I guess," replied Hayden carefully. Flint opened his mouth to speak; however, a commanding call from Brighton dispersed that idea.

"Hendrix! Mitchell! Get over here!"

A few soldiers were walking up and down the trenches as the pair passed, chucking dead bodies of fallen foes and comrades onto a muddy, grimy heap, which slowly rotted as the minutes passed on. Bravo Six centred in a circle beside a large shell crater, watching as smoke lingered around them and rolled down the back of their throats.

"Cole, casualty report." Brighton checked while brushing and patting damp sand off his arms. The lieutenant nodded and took out a burnt sheet of paper, which had names listed down from their platoon.

"Luka Smith, KIA," Cole announced blankly as he scratched his name off the paper. "Ruben Cruz. KIA." The pencil scribbled across the page. "That's all I got, sir."

"Good. Stephen's going home. Anyone else?" Brighton took that as a no. "Hang on, where's Harper?"

Flint traced his memory back and remembered Cruz being the one first to go. "Cruz, sir, is gone as well. Killed back at the landing crafts."

The entire group looked down onto at the ground and slowly, one by one, swiped off their helmets. Hayden sighed and muttered, "So, we only got five left. How are we going to cope with such small numbers, sir?"

"More will come, Private Hendrix. The one definitely staying though is me." Brighton followed up by swiftly pointing out, "Cole, Willis, you and Mitchell. I will inform HQ shortly, if that's okay with you." Flint nodded sharply. "Right then, get your backpacks on and triple-check your rifles. We're heading for the Rhine River through Bayeux in an hour with the 8th Armoured Division. Good luck."

Flint retreated back into the bunker, leaning his M1 Garand against the cracked concrete walls and perching himself so that he could see the beach. The first seagulls appeared, swooping through the clouds and striking downwards, tearing at the bits of rotting human flesh that lay on the sand below. Flint guessed around four hundred had been slain victim to the might of the MG that sat attached next to him. Fumes of gunpowder and death slipping out the circular barrel as Flint, exhausted and deprived, rubbed his eyes. After he had restocked on ammunition and grenades from a nearby group of Yorkshire lads, he set off back to the meeting point. The dead bodies had been thankfully taken away however, blood still sat in great pools around him. Sprawls of rubble too sat in large humps, collecting ash and more stones as workers shovelled more onto the heap.

"Mitchell," called Brighton as Flint glanced back. He noticed that his commander had polished his shoes and buttons as he came gallantly walking forwards.

Flint quickly hooked up his helmet across his head and saluted. "Sir."

"None one of that, private. Think your arms need a rest," said Brighton and chuckled at his own wit. His smile faded away and he sternly stared at Flint. "You okay?"

"As if I had just landed."

Of course, this was an obvious lie caught out by the sergeant who pulled out a pack of cigarettes. "Good...good." He breathed in deeply and lit the first cigarette. "About that incident with the father earlier, it was nothing personal, you did what you had to do, I did what I had to do. Like a circle that comes around."

"What, shooting the man point blank?" Flint replied sourly, almost disgusted by the merciless act. "How many times you done that before, huh?"

"Five years in this war, Flint. Five years in man's biggest conflict. I think that I have no regrets when it comes to ending people's lives." Brighton eyes were like shadows, showing a violent, battle-hardened window, but a light to someone who was horrifically broken inside.

"Just like Chamberlain from Burma, eh?" Flint mumbled. Brighton bit his lip and replied with a simple "Watch it".

9 – Trial by Fire

The soldiers of Bravo Six climbed into the awaiting, empty US Sherman tanks, hearing the clanks of the outer rim as it made contact with their rifles and winding strands of magazines for the LMGs. The M4 Sherman tank was considered one of the most enduring, efficient and all-round best of the medium-sized allied tanks armoury. It had a 6.5-inch reinforced iron armour plating, which covered all areas and was great at stomaching critical hits from the infamous German 'Tiger Tank' that infested western France. Designed in mid-1940, it had a maximum of five crew members, which could sit inside, each one fitted to a certain role, which was extremely important in fighting off a vast enemy. There was the commander, perched at the front, navigating the tanks movements and barrages. Then there was the driver, loader and two machine gunners who sat either side waiting to unleash a deadly storm. Each MG gunner had three hundred rounds fitted to their M1919s and was vital when cranking up to speeds of 30mph through the battlefield. The main, pivoting tank gun could take out an entire building and added the weight of the armoured vehicle to an astonishing thirty-three tons, depending on its variant of course. Finally, it was manufactured dark green with an iconic allies symbol, a white star, on the hood of the vehicle.

Flint descended down to his designated position, which Brighton had assigned him. He was in charge of the main tank gun, responsible for delivering huge, vital hits to enemy forces while also being informed by the shell loader what the enemy positions were. Having a basic idea on how to handle the huge weapon, he realised how small and uncomfortable the inside was. It was crammed with ammo, tank shells and some rusting repair tools, which sat almost claustrophobically in the corner. Flint was in the centre square, high up in a metal chair, which allowed him to use the huge gun. Hayden was on the right MG, while Harry on the left, already feeding the hundreds of killer bullets into the prepped machine. Cole sat below Flint, in charge of loading the main gun while at the same time operating the contact radio system. The crew had an idea that pretty much all escape hope depended on him. Cole had grime and rust streaked across his weary face and he carefully jolted a huge shell into the inner chamber.

"Right, men! We good to go, eh?" Brighton announced rhetorically as his voice echoed through the cramped Sherman. A low murmur of agreement came from the squad apart from Harry, who hummed the song *'We'll meet again'* quietly. He was a very silent person, Harry, however when it came to the real stuff where half a battalion relied on him to save their lives, he was not short of heroics!

The sergeant started up the engine at the front, surrounded by different maps of Bayeux, which too was also surrounded by huge plains and scatters of woodland. Flint's knees and elbows were squeezed together, rubbing against the chair as the tank started to lumber forward terrifically. He felt trapped, terrified of what would happen if they get encircled or, even worse, discover a fire, which would begin to blaze inside. Flint had heard of what the Nazis and Russians used, wine bottles filled with flammable liquids that were lit and thrown inside of tanks; 'Molotov Cocktails' they were. He had heard rumours of men who were smoked up in an inevitably fiery end, locked inside with no mercy. Passing the thought, he hoped for a more calm string of thoughts to roll into his head.

"Hey, Mitchell! Keep your eyes ahead, yeah? Don't want to be ambushed," Harry implied.

Flint nodded, feeling sweat gradually trickling down his forehead as his shirt and trousers became sticky from the lack of air. It was an overcast day, clouds gathered up above menacingly as the sun was snatched away into the midst of near thunderstorms. Apart from the blazing engine at the rear end of the vehicle, he was sweating because of the extreme tension and how warm it was inside the tank. *It is like a furnace!* He thought. Looking out of the slight slit in the armour, he noticed that a convoy of more Shermans joined them, each loaded to the max with joint American-British platoons. Most of the Americans looked battered, bandages tied around their injured or missing limbs. Cole spoke up as he realised the squad had been staring in sorrow, "They've just arrived from Omaha, lads. Apparently, it was the worst down there than it was with us! Two thousand casualties!"

Flint nearly gasped at the figures.

"The closest place is Bayeux and is twenty minutes from here, I suggest you rest now 'cause it's the Germans' closest stronghold from the beaches," Brighton spat. "We're gonna scout it out and engage in any spotted enemy activity. You got that?"

"Yes, sir," the crew replied simply.

The next half-an-hour was riddled with edging tension for the men of Bravo Six. Each individual one wished they could be sent back to their loving and caring families where they belonged instead of this nightmare. Flint saw Cole writing a letter to his wife and kids, hoping them a safe time and comforting them while he was away. *'But first I have to fight, and find, Hitler, and all his associates, which had doomed so many to a brutal and unnecessary death'* were the exact words written in the mood-dampening letter.

The tank convoy rumbled on despite the downcast emotions, the mighty machines shaking as they crossed all types of terrain. Through the mud they pressed on, through the fields they pressed on, through the barbed wire and villages and gardens they still pressed on. Until they reached Bayeux. A simple town it was, Bayeux, a looming forest stood located a mile behind; however, you could still see the leaves of trees horizon because of how low the apartments were. Old-fashioned houses and cobblestone roads greeted the half a dozen M4 Shermans that stumbled upon it. The tanks stopped dead in their tracks by the entrance, waiting to see anything awaiting them. The commanders were starting to contemplate if this was even the right town! It was eerily quiet, only the whistles of wind scraping the shady bushes and starved chickens in the streets were heard. There were only about twenty-five houses in the complex, most consisting of square, stone bungalows that had dry, skeleton-like flowers rooted in front. Built in a basic rectangular form, Bayeux had simple yet lonely streets winding up and down.

"It's abandoned, sir," whispered Hayden in a low trailing voice.

Sergeant Brighton ignored him and the thought, still peering through his opening and leaving a hand hanging in the air to halt any further talking. A sudden noise nearly scared the crew half to death; it definitely made them jump!

However, it was just Brighton's crackling old field telephone.

"Bravo Six, this is Alpha Two! Echo One has been hit and stranded half a mile east from the entrance of Bayeux! We and the rest of the convoy have re-

routed to support and extract the crew...clear the town without us, no enemy
activity has been spotted! Over!"

"Alpha Two, this is Bravo Six, we understand and heading into Bayeux, over," Brighton replied unnaturally worried.

Flint gulped. The chickens had stopped pecking and scurried into the isolated houses, the rotting doors left wide open, allowing anyone to enter. Vines had stemmed their ways across the body of the houses, suffocating any space for valuable life. Flint felt his nerves jangling inside, terror clawing away at any other emotion as he felt himself shuddering rapidly. Harry started whimpering in the dark corner, shaking violently as the events from the beach began to haunt him while the deafening silence still lingered in the air. It was almost as everyone was mute; nothing could be heard. That's when Flint noticed it while staring at the ghost town. There was something odd...laying very still by the side of the street against a fence with blood and bullet-holes all over it. Flint perched his head higher to get a better view. It was a civilian's dead body. Flint breathed in, trying to calm himself, but he couldn't, he can't, he was struggling to contain himself as he knew that one explosion would split him into a hundred pieces. He would be wiped off the face of this earth...

That's when the first cry was heard.

BANG!

Like a tidal wave, Bravo Six's tank was blasted by a thousand bullets, desperately trying to puncture the thick armour as the crew tried to maintain control. Red-hot fragments bounced high inside of the vehicle, hitting Lieutenant Cole in the neck, which squirted out a stream of blood onto Flint's lap. Sparks skimmed the air around them as the crew tried to spot the attackers; but they couldn't see due to the immense pressure and machine gun fire they were under. The noise was terrific inside. Huge thuds and twangs erupted and echoed like a rock concert.

"Flint!" Brighton barked savagely. "Do something!"

"Where are they?!" Flint screamed back. Hayden started firing his tank machine gun, a chain of deadly bullets smacking into the houses and fences as he saw his first frail target. Brighton yanked up at the field telephone, shouting into it as the tank became much weaker by the second. He called in for immediate back up and was done in seconds as he stirred the tank to cover from the blinding enemy guns.

"Cole! Cole! Get up now!" shrieked Flint as he watched helplessly from his high chair. Coughing violently, the lieutenant sat up, blood spilling onto the surface of the tank and flowing over to Hayden. Hayden forced him to switch seats, taking control of loading the gun as he threw Cole into the machine gun chair. Smoke began to fog up all around the Sherman, leaving them disabled, as the Germans grew nearer. The ambush was on a much larger scale now, mortars and grenades rocketing near them. It was like there was nothing they could do. They were surrounded.

"Flint! Get ready!"

But then, to their utter joy, the smoke finally cleared.

Hayden Hendrix eyed the abandoned house opposite the tank, hoping for a glimpse of German soldiers or an artillery team. His wish came true. A pack of soldiers came running with LMGs to the windows; placing them on bipods on the edge, as they vigorously opened fire. Hayden screamed: "Gunners! Two storey building, twelve o'clock! Second floor!" His voice echoed through the tank. Flint took in the coordinates and aimed exactly at the enemies, his heart racing.

"Targets acquired!" Flint shouted just over the intense noise.

"Fire!"

BOOM!

A mighty blow shook the tank as the shell launched forward, absolutely destroying the front of the house as it crumbled to a blistering heap of sinking rubble.

"Good job!" Brighton announced, as some of the fire had been greatly relieved of.

The tank started to make some progress down the road even with it being under constant heavy fire from the looming houses to the sides. Flint felt the raw grind of the engine as it rumbled on, his whole body vibrating, ready to demolish another building. A couple of Germans sprinted across the street with rounds upon rounds of rifle ammo strapped over their shoulders, dodging their men's own bullets. Just before they could make it behind a fence, Cole gunned both down, a storm of deadly bullets bolting into their lifeless bodies. Hayden picked up another heavy iron shell from the rack, letting it side into place. He gave the thumbs up, slamming the shell into the cannon hole, then glanced up once again for visible hostiles.

"Flint! RPG! Two o'clock! Third floor!"

"Quick, let's go! They're ripping us apart in here!" shouted Brighton.

"Target acquired!" Flint assured as the main gun pivoted right towards the section. A lone grenadier was fiddling with his RPG, hoping he had enough time. But the bare reality was that he really didn't.

"Fire!"

BOOM!

Another force shook the tank as the shell blasted off, piercing the edge of a bungalow and sending it toppling down onto some near Germans, as well as the grenadier.

"Flint, again!" cried Hayden as he heaved a huge bullet into the steaming chamber.

"Ready!"

"I'm gonna head up top to the machine gun! Cole, cover me!" yelled Brighton as he yanked the lid open and stuck his head out. A breeze of fresh air descended upon him and gushed into the tank with relief. Hayden gazed through once again, peering for any anti-tank weapons. A charge of assault troops came dashing down the dusty road, dynamite and sticky bombs in their hands. Their faces were petrified as they ran alone at the Sherman.

"Assault team! Down the road, twelve o'clock!"

"Targets acquired!"

"Fire!"

BOOM!

The incoming group were ripped apart into pieces, a mess of bloody legs and arms flew up into the air as a huge crater opened up metres ahead of the tank. A whining sound pierced Flint's ears as he winced at the pain, rubbing his head slowly. Suddenly, under the constant banging, the field telephone rattled forwards. Upon hearing this, Brighton leaped back down into the Sherman and snatched at the telephone.

"I hope you're here to help us!" Brighton boomed infuriatingly into the speaker.

"Bravo Six, this is Foxtrot Nine! Our tanks are on the way! Two mins tops and we'll meet you at the cathedral on the east side of town. Hold in there, over!"

A heavy American accent spoke on the other side. Sergeant Brighton shook his head and stiffly took the controls once more, frequently having to dodge incoming mortar strikes. Huge lumps of cobblestone and earth flew up into the ground around the tank, ear-splitting noises engulfing the smoke and atmosphere. However, they still carried on.

"Willis, drive will you? I'm going up again! We need to get to the cathedral NOW!"

Harry winked whilst Sergeant Brighton reloaded a fresh magazine into his Thompson and burst out the lid. Cole pulled the trigger down all the way, unleashing havoc upon the Germans as Brighton ascended into the open air. He shouted wildly while gunning them down, encouraging himself to show no mercy. A bleeding, young man was crawling to safety, crying while he did so. But that didn't stop Cole. The German was riddled with bullets, sprawled across the pavement in a pool of blood. Brighton positioned himself on the MG on the hood of the tank, loading a huge clip of 250 bullets into the chamber and drawing it violently back.

"Cover me!" barked the sergeant.

He fired the massive machine gun, bullets flying in all directions as he scattered the many foes down. The tank sped forward smashing a sandbag barricade into a million different chippings. They ignored all the fire raining down onto the Sherman, only focussing on getting to the cathedral for aid. Flint watched as his surroundings swept past him, desolate houses, fences, gates, walls all zooming past by the shear rush of the crew. He tasted the sour oil in the back of his throat, and had to continuously swipe rust and sweat from his face as they dashed forward along the cracked roads. The tank took a very sharp turn left, swaying all the men drastically to the side. The noise from the MGs never stopped, Harry and Cole were firing tirelessly away at the seemingly never-ending ambushing soldiers. Finally, after a near contact with an RPG, which was quickly dealt with by Flint, they spotted above the houses a large spiked structure that enlightened them with hope. It was the cathedral.

"Bravo Six to Foxtrot Nine, we see the cathedral! Where are you guys, over?" Harry yelled into the field telephone.

"Foxtrot Nine to Bravo Six, we're by the left entrance of the cathedral. A friendly artillery strike has been called in on your position. I repeat a friendly artillery strike has been called in on your position in T-minus fifteen seconds, over."

"Wait? What! Fifteen seconds!" Flint howled in defeat.

"You heard that Mitchell! We need to get outta here! Only a few more blocks 'til the safe zone!" cried the sergeant from above.

Harry stamped his foot down, smoke funnelling out from the exhausts as the Sherman leapt forward once more, crushing any obstacles in its path. Suddenly, an immense barrage of shells shattered the town's houses behind them, a chaotic terrain of falling bombs and smoke battering the area. Brighton fell back into the tank, his head banging against the main loading chamber. Multiple bungalows crumbled to the ground and the road blew into several pieces as the shells kept coming, annihilating the cracked tar.

"Flint, more gunners west! Second building behind the store, first floor!" declared Hayden. He then added quickly, "Harry! Stop the tank, now!"

Harry halted and Flint gazed out of the hatch seeing a trio of scruffy, regular German soldiers throwing stick bombs, which bounced off the tank, rocking the earth around them as they imploded. The bullets never seemed to stop coming, tiny cracks and holes started to weave slightly open, as the tank was getting much weaker. An abandoned corner shop, *La Chocolatiere Du Panier*, rotted in front of the spotted axis soldiers. Old sweet jars and plastic wrappings littered across the wooden boards, which collected cobwebs and dust.

"I see it, Hayden!" Flint declared as he lined up the shot, the huge mechanical barrel spinning towards the target.

"Fire!"

BOOM!

Once more, the tank sprung back, a deafening noise erupting across the hectic Bayeux. *La Chocolatiere Du Panier* was hit by the shell, not the enemy. The whole chocolate shop slanted to the side before crumbling into a messy heap of debris and dirt like a house after an earthquake. The Germans grinned to themselves as they galloped away, thankful for avoiding a sudden death.

"We missed!" Flint alerted, weary to the idea that they could be the Germans who could blow this tank up. And they would be.

I manage to climb over the descending rubble, frequently dodging huge sheets of rock cascading down as I fight on for the Fatherland. Tragically, I had seen Wilhelm crushed by the incoming debris, his fate left not to spare by his own will. We had fought the world together – me and him. Against the pushing Soviets and Polish. But now he had fallen, let him rest. I throw myself behind a heap of bricks, hoping that they would be my cover and a safe place to shoot from. Resting my Karabiner 98 against the bloodied debris, I glance at the main tank slit, wishing for a clean shot to the skull if the lucky opportunity arises. Whilst aiming down the iron sights, I notice how much I am shaking, the gun almost rocking in my hand. I force myself to calm down. To focus on what lays ahead.

"Ferdinand! Take this incendiary!"

I look to my right, seeing Stefan reluctantly passing me a bottle. I nod in agreement under the constant drum-like and excruciatingly painful sounds. A scatter of turret fire blasts my way and blows Stefan's leg off as more lead ricochets off the broken walls around us. He rolls around in pain, yelping words of mercy; but the bullets never stop coming. Taking out my medical pack, my heart freezes as my now dead comrade gazes into the sky, as if feeling lucky and hoping for a better life for us. Clenching my bruised fist in rage, I light the bottle he gave me and launch it over to the tank in an athletic manner. It bursts into flames on the underside of the Sherman. A flame ignites. Screaming and horrendous echoing shouts can be heard as those doomed allied soldiers try to escape. Smoke funnels out the lid as my men begin to come out of their defensive ditches and surround the vehicle, hoping for an easy route to undoubtable victory.

Groaning in agony, Flint realised that both his worst nightmares had come true. They had been encircled and smoked out at the same time like foxes. He leapt out of his high iron chair and onto the oily floor of the tank. Thousands of sparks ushered into his face and melted off his cheeks. Cole, Hayden and Brighton were shrieking commands and heaving themselves closer to the lid where their only chance to live lay. Clouds of smoke engulfed around them like fog and soon Flint began to choke, splutters of pain and soot exiting his throat.

He banged into a MG and stumbled down, coughing in oil, and crawled. Light-headed and battered, Flint glanced above him as Harry managed to lift himself out of the burning, steaming vehicle.

Cries are heard as the lid flaps open, revealing a petrified, scarred medic as he hurls himself out the tank. The man sticks his arms out, surrendering. He is met full-force by a wave of bullets, blood spilling from various holes in his chest as he tumbles back into the Sherman in a slow statue-like position. I feel my rifle crack at him while he tumbles down, more holes ripping in his clothes.

Roasting alive, Flint and Hayden's boots ignited into flames, dissolving the leather as they tried once more to exit. It was like being in a thousand-degree furnace, their bodies boiling whilst they try to scramble out. Harry's corpse, which was bullet-ridden and soaking in crimson red, crunched Brighton to the leaking floor, lifelessly staring into Flint's eyes. Yet another obstacle to climb against.

"We gotta get outta here!" someone shrieked.

Footsteps and German commands were heard as the enemy climbed onto the tank, investigating and preparing to shoot if what was left of Bravo Six decided to come out. All hope of escape and life flooded out of Flint. The certainty of despair and loss overwhelmed him and caused him to shed a single tear. All of them rested, exhausted, against the walls and accepted their fate. The crackling flames ascending towards them grew hotter and larger, slowly barrelling forwards.

"This is the end, boys," quoted Cole, who was still clutching his slit and bleeding neck.

Smoke and ash devoured them until they were practically invisible, rolling eerily down their lungs. Suddenly like light after a storm, the telephone crackled on, buffering as it delivered hope to the trapped victims.

"Bravo Six, this is Alpha Two! We see your Sherman stranded in the middle of the road. German forces are crawling all over it! Permission to engage? Over!"

Flint crawled towards the telephone through the mess of fire, oil and blood, his last hope to live. The communication device was melting, a lava-like substance peeling off the black edges.

"Alpha…Alpha Two, you there?" he just managed to splutter.

"Standing by, over."

"Get those Germans off our tank…"

A massive burst of MG fire from Alpha Two scattered into the soldiers above and obliterated some as they leaped off, horrified by the new hidden tank that had just appeared. Blood dripped into the Sherman, the lid now slightly open.

"Go! Now!" Brighton shrieked as he used the last of his energy to heave himself out the tank. His pistol blasted in his hands as he rapidly fired shots, leaping down by the side of the vehicle. Flint followed. The fires shimmered in his bloodshot eyes as he stumbled out cluelessly.

I throw myself off the tank as a hail of blistering bullets comes zipping into my comrades. I dash through the smoke to the nearest building, half a motel crumpled on the ground. Throwing grenades while I retreat, huge clumps of earth and concrete blast up metres from me. My eyes are covered in mud and ash yet I run on through the bullets.

Flint felt a fresh breeze of air sweep across his face as his coat flapped in the wind, a cold, tense feeling unravelling him. His M1 Garand was waiting patiently in his hands; the magazine fully loaded however severely burnt. Spying a lone German retreating back to his defensive area, a boil of pure hatred hardened Flint as he pointed the rifle at the running Nazi. The German's head lay perfectly in his sights crosshair. Without hesitating, he felt the curve of the trigger split in his hands, a killer bolt of metal steering into the back of the German's neck. The man collapsed forwards, his face in a distorted surprise, face flat onto the torn concrete. Blood slowly seeped from his neck.

The last thing I will ever feel is the cold yet satisfying wind across my back, the overcast sky above gathers for celebration of my departure away from this horrific war and away from life itself. My warmth and thoughts fades. My time has come…

10 – Candlelight Fields

Depleted and scarred, the final men of Bravo Six trudged in the darkness through to their sleeping areas. It was a two-storey house with a basic design, two bedrooms, a kitchen, toilet and dining room. Yet since it was abandoned, they simply decided to sleep by the main entrance – or what was left of it. Flint was lying outside against a broken and bullet-ridden stairway; his blistered feet surrounded by rusty sheets of metal and crushed bricks. He felt the night air breeze upon him, the atmosphere deeply clear as he gazed up at the millions of stars above; feeling a slight connection to how it was back in ordinary England. They were on the same war-torn street they fought on earlier, little patches of fire and sparks could still be seen glistening in the heavy darkness. The only movement was those off the mechanics who were working tirelessly on the broken and smashed Sherman tank, oil and grease rubbed around their weary faces. The frequent sound of spanners and drills were heard softly, just beyond the calm wind against the trees. Chatters of hope and hysterical laughing echoed inside the house. Candles were neatly lit as silhouettes of Hayden and Brighton could both be seen drinking away on whiskey found in the rotting cupboards. Lieutenant Cole was due back in a few months due to his slit neck, but for the moment, it was just the three of them left. They were expected to receive more reinforcements soon.

Bundling himself in his light green camo overalls, Flint rested on his helmet, exhausted and painfully aching. He just managed to shut his eyes when a deep voice rumbled close to him.

"You gotta dead Kraut next to you, you know."

Flint bolted upright suddenly, snatching out a slender pistol swiftly.

"Hey, come on now; put the gun away, do I really look like one of them to you?" The figure nodded to the dead German corpse, which Flint hadn't seen.

The man had an unmissable southern American accent, which sounded like a stereotypical cowboy, his outline giving a tall and quite bulky being. Flint lowered his gun with a humble expression in the dark and hid it back in his back trouser; ashamed to be so unaware of whom he was pointing his weapon at so easily. The soldier levelled himself with Flint, crouching on the discarded rubble and staring into the clear distance.

"Is this is what we fight for? Peace? It feels pretty good to be out of the firing line for a bit," muttered the American. Flint agreed.

The pair sat silently in the night rays, feeling the warmth of rest descending upon one another.

"Spare a candle, mate. It's starting to freeze out here," Flint said willingly.

The man took out a singular but small, wax candle, past liquids half way from dripping off the sides. He then took out an ancient matchbox and struck the stick, before lighting the candle, which lit into a small, hopeful flame of heat.

"You're the squad leader of Foxtrot Nine, right?"

"Yeah, I guess I am now, we lost our previous one down at the fields earlier. Went up to the main MG on the roof, came down in several pieces. Good friend." The man's eyes strained, looking away from Flint's eyes and wiping a hand over his ashen face.

"Flint Mitchell." He spoke with a firm handshake.

"Doug Campbell," the muttered reply was.

Flint had his first look at him under the light, Campbell, a long-ragged scar dragged from his left eye to his cheek and his eyes were similar to Brighton's, traumatised. He had jet-black hair trimmed short, with sodden bandages strapped across his muscular limbs in a careless fashion.

"How many you guys lost since you started?"

"Four outta nine." Flint sighed.

"Well, you're gonna have to muster up what you have. New reinforcements coming in only tomorrow evening!" he pronounced worryingly. Campbell peered at the just visible mechanics who called it a day, wiping sweat and grease from their chins as they settled into the nearby residence. "Our divisions are pushing further east at dawn; to La Colline aux Oiseaux or something." He chuckled. "Gonna be a tough one. Hitler's got strongholds all over that sector."

"Yeah? How many?"

"We don't know yet, probably be 'round a few hundred," he remarked. A shocked expression unravelled across Flint's face and his heart stopped. Biting his lip, he finally arose and headed for his sleeping bunk after saying his farewells to Campbell…

"We'll do what we can."

First light ascended across Bayeux, shimmers and streaks of rays glided down to another day of combat. Brighton was first out, glancing at the mended tank next to a rusty fence before trudging to the armoured jeeps. He took his map out and blew the dust, revealing only some dotted lines pointed at a lone field. The others woke up, aching from the previous day and limping as they came over to their sergeant. Piling into the jeeps, Flint perched himself at the rear with a Bren LMG. It weighed him down however it was a very powerful weapon indeed. The magazine stuck out from the top and was widely recognised around the globe. He juddered as the jeep started to slowly move.

"You know where we going?" Hayden asked as he rubbed his eyes across his sleeves.

"I don't know. Something 'bout us going against some strongholds again," Flint replied.

"Great."

Hayden sipped from his canteen. Out of nowhere, a huge rumbling convoy of allied trucks came revving down the main road, crushing over loose bricks and fences. They came to a stuttering halt behind Flint.

"You guys the ones heading north-east?" called a soldier from behind the steering wheel. Flint watched as Brighton jogged around the jeep and replied to the officer through the window.

"Yeah. We gonna hit the stronghold in fifteen minutes."

"We're coming with, we've got about seventy men in these trucks," the soldier then added whilst adjusting the straps on his helmet. "All right, let's move." Ten jeeps drifted out of Bayeux as Flint sat anxious in his exposed position, driving closer to their main objective…the Rhine.

After a while they stopped on the side of an abandoned little country road, potholes riddling it and stray pigeons encircling. Deep, dark green trees were sprawled around in clumps and shrubs littered their surroundings. A field lay in front, a basic short trimmed spread that went on for many miles. Wind swept across them and rustled some nearby leaves creating a miniature whirlwind, the noise almost catching the men off guard for a moment. Flint Mitchell leaped off the side of the truck, leaving the Bren unused sitting attached to the jeep. Hayden followed him, all checking their rifles and handguns. Brighton spoke a few words to the driver and left, all the jeeps making a U-turn and striding back to Bayeux for more men. Around eighty British soldiers were gathered along the tiny road, crouching and peering through the leaves to the field. The tree line that loomed above lay in great cover, providing you to see out but not in. Over to their right in the distance was a small farmhouse with multiple windows, the main barn door still left gaping open.

"Delta Company! Nearest Nazi stronghold is about two miles that way…" Brighton hand-signalled towards the field. "…Sergeant Lidgeberry, your squad sticks with us. Sergeant Raymond, head left, and Colonel Warren, right. The rest strike the middle with me and Lidgeberry. Don't stumble and keep both eyes wide open. Don't make a mess of this, let's move…"

The whole company revealed itself and emerged from the treeline, nearly a hundred Brits began to pace forward across the field. Flint was next to Hayden, shaking at the hand as they pressed on. The only thing heard was the whoosh of the wind and the jangling of their ammo belts and helmets, the silence nearly too frightening to handle.

"Watch the farmhouse," whispered Hayden intriguingly. Flint eyed the red barn in the distance as it sat worthless in between the spreads of vegetation. The mud squelched below Flint's feet, but he didn't notice; his eyes were constantly fixed on the horizon, the clouds beginning to stir up above into a moody grey. The large scatter of British troops would be hard to counter in flat terrain like this.

So they had mistaken.

"*Feuer!*"

RATATA!

A blistering hail of bullets spiralled in from an unseen trench fifty metres in front, taking the whole company by complete and utter surprise.

"Get down!"

The British immediately hurled themselves to the floor in fear. The entire front line peppered with metal that cut straight through them like cheese.

"Ambush! *Ambush!*"

The soldier in front was flung back into Flint, his elbow smacking him in the nose and tossing him down.

"Get up and move!"

Everyone stuck to staying on ground; even the mortar teams dozens of metres away did so too. Hayden glanced to his left and saw three men shot to bits as they spun to the side, their cries muffled under the sudden immense gunfire.

"Run!" screamed Brighton.

Mortar strikes slowly began to rain down, obliterating soldiers around Flint as he slowly staggered back up. Screams of pain and help shook the field as Flint limped and jumped into the nearest crater. Bullets zipped past and went straight through a medic's arm next to Flint, his pleading evaporated as a nearby mortar strike took his life. A radioman crashed into the crater too, his uniform scruffy and muddy as he reached for the field telephone.

"Delta 3 to Alpha-minor, this is Delta Company, we request immediate artillery support now! 1-5-2-1, hundred metres from the initial tree line, over!" he shouted. It was an order rather than a request.

Flint winked in appreciation.

"Forget the confirmation! Just bomb!" drained the radioman almost rapping due to how fast he spoke back into the telephone.

"That should hold 'em off!" barked Flint. Before the radioman could reply a short snap of rifle fire cracked through his chest and out his spine, leaving him bleeding and sobbing around the rim of the crater.

The constant thudding and booming of nearby bombs whirred in Flint's ears as he dashed over and forward. The ground had now become a rocky landscape from the conflict and they finally had cover through the midst of the chaos. Flint bumped into another soldier and crunched onto the ground, a killer burst of bullets whizzing overhead and chucking the ground up beside him.

"Forward! Forward!" shrieked Hayden as he knelt behind a mound of dead bodies, the bullets still splatting through.

He raised his gun up and shot twice, pelting a German with two bullets to the thigh and chest. The enemy was coming into view now, slowly advancing and lining up MG42 rounds towards the British. Their grey helmets could be seen bobbing up and down behind cover.

"Somebody help me!" wailed a gunner who'd been hit.

A hand-grenade tumbled under Flint's knee. In a flash, he just managed to throw it back, taking out a running German with it. Aiming at a solitary soldier, Flint fired the gun in his hands rapidly, bullets bolting as they sliced through the dark grey trench coats of the axis. Flint saw more…and shot. A line of Germans came scrambling from a torn crater, petrified as they strode forward. Flint fired his Garand over a dozen times, their blood spitting out onto the floor as half of them fell back into the crater. Suddenly, one came bustling towards Flint with a knife, but with mightily quick reflexes, Flint skid to the side and smacked him with his rifle, whipping out a handgun to finish him off. Hayden burst forward dodging bullets as he slipped and leaned his back against a ditch. He looked over to his right and spotted a medic attending a severely wounded man in the open with bullets skimming just around his feet. "Yes, our barrage finally!" cried Hayden in joy as he heard the whistling and streams of smoking shells trailing through the sky.

A chain of explosions rocked the earth. Germans were chucked into the air, most body parts with. Brighton peered and stuck his rifle on the edge of a new crater, picking of the screaming Germans carefully. Mud splashed in his face as reloaded his magazine. The entirety of Baker Eleven suddenly came running from his left flank, naive to the fact that a whole trench line of German rifleman were waiting just in front.

"Get back! They see you!" Flint shrieked under the mortar strikes and gunfire. The Germans spotted Baker Eleven and made it look like an easy shooting range, each one headshot as they desperately sought for cover. Sergeant Lidgeberry pivoted back to distract them by tossing a couple of grenades however a storm of bullets shot straight through him, zipping into the mud. He stumbled and collapsed like a brick wall to the smearing mud. The flametrooper from back at Sword beach trod next to Flint, a strong smell of gas lingering around him.

"That thing still work?" demanded Flint, knowing it could take out the entire trench line.

"Enough to burn a thousand of 'em!" he replied almost joyful at the glistening thought.

Flint signalled the trench line to him, nearly killed as he did so! With a simple nod, the flametrooper lumbered forward, the heavy canisters weighing him fully down. A charge came from the British, supporting the lone attacker who prepared the flamethrower. Smoke raised up around him as Flint cover fired, shooting dozens of bullets into the Germans' bodies. The desolate trooper had the ground and snatched the trigger.

BANG! BANG! BANG!

Just as the first spit of fire came streaming out, a rival assault trooper spotted the flametrooper and burst a dozen bullets into his stomach. He fell to his knees, as if showing honour and felt the bullets penetrate the fuel canisters.

BOOM!

The flametrooper shattered into a thousand pieces as a fierce uproar of fire came blasting towards Flint. He evaded the wave as he stumbled right, all around him his comrades lined with scattering shots of enemy MGs. His face was mortified as a German charge erupted. He ducked into a ditch as they did so; hearing the aggressive roar and clash of bayonets as he crawled through the soaking mud. Dead British soldiers constantly fell on him as he steadied his rifle, pointing it at the Germans who plunged blades into English stomachs. Gazing down the iron sights, a splash of blood rained over him, but it did not interrupt as he slammed a round full of bullets at the nearest German. Another mortar explosion rocked the earth metres away flinging him into a fellow soldier. They both smacked into each other and tumbled to the ground.

"You okay?" muttered the soldier. Dark black hair was sprawled with sweat down his forehead as an exhausted face greeted him.

"I'm—"

BOOM!

A long, slim edge of shrapnel pierced the other man's chest, before another piece split into his own arm!

"Medic!" howled Flint.

Flint dragged him across the mud with bullets smacking into the ground around them. Using the last sap of energy, he rolled the severely injured soldier into a steaming crater. Flint put him into a position for treatment, desperately aiding his wounds as the man recited muddled-up and random words. His body jittered violently as he spotted a bullet-hole on his thigh, blood flowing by the second. *He must've been shot while I was dragging him!* With muddy hands soaked in fresh blood and despite the hectic battle around him, Flint quoted: "Look! The medic's on his way!" The soldier's eyes flashed with hope then despair as another wave of pain ushered through him. There wasn't an actual medic coming, but it had calmed the man down. Flint took out his medical kit and wrapped the bandages around his chest, comforting him with stories of back in London as he did so.

"You're doing good. What's your name?" Flint whispered thoughtfully as he stopped the bleeding from both sources. The soldier managed to smile limp and reached for his trouser pocket as he did so.

"Daniels…Cooper Daniels. And give…this to my brother," he spluttered hopelessly.

"No need, give it yourself when you go back. I got you," Flint reassured.

Cooper outstretched his hand, a little pre-war picture of his brother with him strolling by a lake in Hawaii. Mesmerised, Flint reached to take it gently wanting to treasure the image. A sudden chatter of fire darted into the crater and both men ducked for cover; Flint lay on top to protect him and felt the heat skim his back. Dirt rained on them like a vicious wave of whistling hail.

"You're good now, don't worry you're getting outta here!" Flint stated as he crawled over to his backpack on the opposite side of the ditch.

"Thank you!" Cooper started laughing, grateful to be able to gain a painful ticket home.

BOOM!

A mighty force slammed Flint into the ditch's wall.

His heart stopping.

Ears ringing.

He was hearing in whining, faint ways in which he had never suffered with before. He didn't care about himself but only of what happened to Cooper. The flashbacks re-emerged…all he could remember was home with his father, living in a peace which no violence like this had ever bothered him. And then reality caught up. An agonising shriek blurted out. To start off with, Flint did nothing at all. His head spun as eyes set itself on the ghastly sight before him. He limped up…but crippled down again as his legs couldn't take the strain.

He witnessed the battle around him as the Germans pushed on brutally through the field. Without any reaction from Flint, a war-torn squad of Germans looked down into the ditch. The only sight, a helmetless young man crawling to a dead soldier perched up against the rim with no arm. One soldier raised his gun – an MP40.

BANG!

The German fell into the ditch headfirst, his comrades suddenly were torn to shreds as Brighton came striding towards them with his trusty Thompson strapped across his back. Another British soldier could be seen next to him hustling with a muddy rifle. He grabbed Flint's arm and hurled him over the edge of the ditch.

"Get up, now!" commanded Brighton. The reply was a nod and quick scramble for a rifle. "Stop fooling about with wounded men! You're not a med—"

"There was no one to help hi—"

"Shut up! Now get back up there and **fight!**"

Flint ignored the hurl of hatred and looked over to Cooper who lay dead in the steaming crater. The mortar shell had finished him off. Even though no physical damage could be seen, his eyes were tightly shut and face pale. His lifeless hand still had the memoir photo clenched inside.

A vain vendetta for Germans brewed inside Flint.

"We have to put distance between us and them!" Hayden snapped.

Flint realised he was back to being able to get killed and peered down the greasy iron sights of his rifle.

"You're right. They're rushing up real quick," he replied with one eye closed. Both of them pinpointed their shots through a growing mist, carefully sniping various enemies that came sprinting through.

"Good shot, mate!" Hayden called.

A loud, grumbling noise slowly graduated among them. Squeaky sounds and a fearful aroma to jump lifted from behind Flint. When he looked back into the sun's rays, an entire silhouette of a Sherman tank loomed over a few metres away.

"Move!" Flint shouted as he clambered out the way of its chugging rails. The tank was almost bouncing through the rocky terrain, the tracks close to skidding off its treads. The main commander sat viciously firing the exposed machine gun; Flint recognised him upon sight. It was Doug Campbell, the American he had encountered recently. A sudden burst of shots smacked into the main body of the tank, but it was only little sparks that peeled off. Campbell looked down onto Flint and Brighton who were manning crucial shots at the Germans.

"Where the cowards at?" the commander bellowed. His black hair flickered in the wind, long strands swinging.

"Trench line to our right! Twenty metres!" answered Brighton. Campbell spotted them in the hidden trench, carrying boxes on boxes of ammunition to the main machine gunners who blasted the British infantry away.

"Foxtrot Nine engage, trench line twenty yards down!" he shrieked into the echoing tank. The battle suddenly paused.

It ferociously kick started again as the tank shell boomed into the firing line. Clouds of dust and ash rose up in the air. Flint sought an entire Nazi battalion gaining ground on his left, trying to dodge out the way of incoming tank shells, their howls were desolate, all stuttering at the wounded radioman to call in reinforcements. They tossed vast amounts of hand grenades into the air taking out several men and leaving most limbless; groaning in agony with mud and blood streaked across their faces.

"There goes our left flank!" Brighton yelled nervously as he retreated into further craters.

"I got 'em," muttered Campbell whilst loading his machine gun on the tank.

RATATATA!

Campbell sprayed lightning bullets towards the advancing axis force. Immeasurable amounts of Germans tumbled to the grimy field as blood came spitting out. The Germans fell into the grass for cover, desperately scrambling down to disappear and not get killed or ripped to bits. The American continued.

"In the open!" he shrieked.

"Mitchell! Hendrix! Get over here!" Brighton ordered as he gunned down an approaching soldier. Flint was glad to get out the line of fire as he steadily retreated back towards Brighton. The drumming now had descended into cracks and booms, something of which occurred at firework nights. He was also glad to see Hayden still alive…but slightly banged up with sludge on bruises. On the other hand, however, his thankfulness became sorrow as Brighton ordered a joint operation with Charlie Eight.

"We need to take that farmhouse now before the German reinforcements set up machine gun nests there…it's gonna be a whole new assault with triple the casualties if we go and hit it later. It's now or never. Let's get it done," Brighton commanded. "Go!"

Hayden, Flint and Brighton along with Charlie Eight wandered behind the main frontline – and whipped right. The other Delta Company squad had seven members – Sergeant Raymond, Miller, Blackwell, Sanders, Heaton, Adler and Wingate; the majority all of which were new to the war. All were constantly petrified for snipers from the main battle and ran as quickly as they could, heaving their gear, which trailed through the grass. They were only fifty metres from the farmhouse when suddenly the soldier next to Flint, Wingate, heard a faint clicking noise beneath his foot.

"What was that?" Heaton anticipated.

"Guys…" Wingate moaned, holding back the dread in his expressions.

Brighton and Charlie Eight's Sergeant Raymond looked back, a stressed expression of deep emotion scarred across their faces. It was an S-Mine – or as the Americans called it, a 'Bouncing Betty', they were heavily used throughout the war against allied infantry and a key trap the Germans used when they retreated out the west of France. They urged him not to move; to let them deal with it. Listening intently, Wingate stood completely still for a reasonable time, the sweat clung on to his curly hair, he was getting too shaky and the longer he stayed, the more nervous he became. He just wanted to quickly try his luck.

"All of you get back, I'm gonna jump," exclaimed Wingate. It was met by a low murmur of disagreement.

"Don't you even dare move!" called an agitated Private Bryan Adler.

Everyone took a few steps back; Brighton tried to tell him that it was going to get him killed. Flint opened his mouth to help, but Wingate leaped into the sodden grass.

BOOM!

His body descended into thin air and morphed into a cloud of mist as Flint rocked back. The deep thud of the explosion from the hidden mine rung in his ears. Vision detained. Eyes closed. It was a few moments when the natural feeling returned. He slowly picked himself up off the ground and shook the dust off his uniform, disgusted by the way death had just been carried out.

"Everyone good?" asked Brighton as he aimed his gun at the farmhouse. A silent yet simple nod from everyone kick started the way back to their objective again.

"What just happened?" Sanders cried as he picked himself out the grass.

Nobody bothered answering. There was nothing to say. The battle still raged on in the centre of the field, huge skyscrapers of red smoke emerged above into the dark, hellish skies.

After pacing across the grass with all their kit, they finally managed to arrive at the worn-out farmhouse. It was a classic compound; a ragged basic red barn filled with hay, buckets, stables, and to the side, stood three small sheds scattered out collecting cobwebs and dirt as if begging for some sort of valuable life. Little puddles started to appear in the cracks of the ancient concrete ground like a sponge, rain dripped in from the morning sky. The lone squad leaned their backs against the main farmhouse's exterior walls, looking back at the misery in the field. Flint wiped the trickling rain from his eyes.

"Double-time, line up!" spoke Raymond.

WHOOSH!

A sudden disturbance erupted from the open window above Flint's head on. He spied a long cylinder trailing through the drizzle, which blasted into Campbell's Sherman. The tank was taken off its axis, slamming into the mud and soldiers beside it. Seconds later, a vicious explosion erupted and rained sheets of metal onto the battlefield. Campbell was gone.

"What…what was that! They just took out our only tank!" Flint howled in horror.

"Get down! They gotta a Panzerfaust on the second floor!" Adler said panting.

Hayden bellowed, "What's a Panzerfaust?" as he leaned towards Adler.

"A bazooka, you fool!" he rebuked. Hayden's face twisted in despair and dread.

"Blackwell, head to the first shed with Miller and secure it! Don't let him see you!"

Raymond ordered as he poked his head around the corner of the farmhouse. Miller and Blackwell nodded, bursting into the open concrete towards the shed opposite whilst holding their helmets on their heads. Two cracks were heard and blood spat out from Miller's back and chest, the bullets zipped in and out in quick succession. Miller crumpled to the ground slowly and miserably.

"Sniper in the window on your right!" Raymond shouted, obviously disturbed.

Blackwell halted. He looked back at his friend paralysed in pain and shock in the rain. Blackwell bolted back to him, holding his camouflaged helmet once more for cover as he did so. He grabbed Miller's backpack and dragged him through puddles to safety, blood streaming across the dull concrete and slowly dissipating in the rain.

"It's just one guy. Must be a commando!" Sanders said and humphed.

"Stay quiet!" Brighton snapped. "He might not be the only one!"

"He's got a Karabiner 98. I remember it on a firing range."

Hayden leaned back and whispered to Flint, "How he fired those two shots so quickly only he would know."

"Private Adler! Get out there and help 'em, we'll cover you!" Sergeant Brighton yelled. Flint aimed at another open window, which sat facing the main road where the other pair were stationed.

"Roger that, Sarge."

A sudden bright white flash appeared as he ran towards the bleeding Miller. Adler's body awkwardly spun sideways, a thin small bullet rocked into his chest. Flint saw this and shot through the window instantly, his gun recoiling back further than expected. The flash disappeared as the sniper slowly fell out of view...preferably into a wet clump of hay. Miller gnashed his teeth in agony as Blackwell bandaged the two shots, bottled water splashing onto his deep wounds. Bryan Adlers's body lay still on the bloodied ground metres away, a pool of crimson liquid streaming around him.

"Keep searching!" exclaimed Brighton.

Flint and Hayden, along with other Charlie Eight soldiers, checked the farmhouse. Nothing seemed remotely out of place. Just rotting crates in the corner and stacks of hay scattered around. The frequent drip seeping from the cracked ceiling splashed onto the dead sniper's body. Flint automatically picked up the sound of the remaining soldiers shotgunning the shed doors outside. All was clear. The initial decision was to stay and rest in the farmhouse until the main battle deceased...that is if they won...

Half an hour passed and the guns in the distance and rocking of the artillery strikes had finally slowly descended. It left only the faint chiming of the small farmer's clock on the wall to make up for the sound. It was only an hour after, however, when the exhausted, battered men arrived at the stables and sheds. They were only around thirty now. It would've been less if reinforcements hadn't been called in the midst of battle. Some were silent, gazing in lost despair at the sights of their fallen brothers, whilst others carried on, even laughing, commenting that it was 'just the same old job'. The casualties were laid down in the red barn house and given their fair share of precious morphine. Strained medics were often seen shaking their heads at the loss of another man, reading their pocket Bibles to the closest friends. More, however, were still being stretchered in on great numbers, the bearers stained with the common sight of blood-clotted uniforms as they heaved the forsaken men to the medical stations – the first two sheds.

It wasn't even five minutes later, when a familiar droning sound on the mid-day horizon steadily approached them. Flint sat up from his clump of hay and walked outside into the rain once again. It was an engine. And not just one engine. Four.

"They're Messerschmitts! Run!" someone boomed in the farmhouse. This sparked severe panic, which spread like uncontrolled wild fire. Four Nazi Messerschmitt Bf 109s came roaming in from the distance, each having its own dynamic sound. With over 34,000 of these fighter planes manufactured in the war, it wasn't going to be uncommon for the battalion to stroll across them. Ever since the shipwreck of the British coast, Flint hated the very sight of those Nazi air machines. They were like wasps to him, no purpose but to hurt. The Messerschmitt could propel at a top speed of 400mph, and the one's incoming on Flint's position was not far off from that velocity. Flint noticed one struggling, like trying to control a wild horse. It had a ripped wing, fuel streaming out along with thin lines of smoke into the clouds.

A sudden bolt of huge rounds zipped into the sheds beside Flint; clattering metal launched in the air as soldiers came stumbling out deeply surprised. The very dirt was shot into the air; sprinkles of concrete and dust slowly blanketing as the rain continued to fall hazily. More streams of bullets came bashing into the ground boosting men up. The fighter planes came roaring over finally, unleashing a deep grumbling noise, which spread fear like wild fire between the shocked British. They were deploying bombs, dozens of them.

"Get out of the barn!" Flint alerted, seeing the mini dots gradually become increasingly larger.

He grabbed his wet M1 Garand and ran. But there was a problem. And it was quite a big one. The planes had been misunderstood. They were actually British Spitfires retreating from a previous dogfight. It explained why one had a ripped wing. He opened his mouth to speak but it was too late. The farmhouse had already burst into a million fiery pieces along with all the wounded, unable men and their medic. He gasped as the Spitfires looped around through the dark clouds and turned sharply for another run. Flint could already imagine the pilots talking as he dashed into the open field. *Drop the second batch on those Germans, lads,* he thought. But why would they strike their own?

"Sergeant, thank goodness, what's happening?" Flint asked as Brighton caught up with him in the empty plain.

"Well, those planes are ours. Word has it some hidden Nazi AA-Gun popped them off just down the road near the forest." He took in a gulp of air. "Intel went bust and they came here and spotted us shooting in the rain. They probably took a wild guess 'cause of the conditions. Looks like it hasn't turned out on our side so well," he stated whilst watching the Spitfires swing back. The engine roared as it skimmed past the burning wreckage of the flaming farmhouse. A radioman came sprinting towards Flint, his backpack jangling as he rested on a wet shrub.

"That thing still work?" called Flint. "We need to tell the air boys."

"Sorry mate." The middle-aged male took in an irregular breath. "It got hit by a piece of shrapnel earlier. Saved my life!" He wearily took it off his shoulders and placed it on his lap. A large metal object pierced out unusually to one side. A cascading bombing noise erupted suddenly behind them as the last run of deadly packages had been released. Flint gulped at the amount of shells that had been dropped and had to take a few steps back due to the heat. Now he knew what it would be like to be German.

"We have to help!" Brighton approached as he and Flint ran.

Into the fire.

11 – The Iron Wall

23 DECEMBER
1944

Fire. That was it. All what was wanted.

Now as they sit here, hearing the whistle and echoing of the artillery guns in the distance, they wonder. Wonder of the warm summer days back home as their skin crawls with desolate shivers and the powerful, blistering cold. Some had hiked in Canada, most the midlands back in Britain; but no one had ever felt that raw chill as those December weeks at the Battle of the Bulge.

Flint Mitchell and Hayden Hendrix lay perched and bundled up in their muddy trench coats and jumpers, the very feeling of their limbs fading away to the endless numbness. Together, they shivered whilst sharing a foxhole on the main Flemish Ardennes line, puffs of white air slipping out every time they took a single breath. A huge yet simple forest loomed over them, the kind that's never dense but spreads over a long, gruelling distance. Slim but overly sized trees were scattered around the various dotted foxholes, iced bits of bark slowly descending down as twigs reluctantly fell beneath the snow-covered canopy. There were hundreds of little foxholes over the entire stretch of the forest, around 55,000 British soldiers fought in the struggle against the Ardennes offensive in France, Belgium and Luxembourg. This specific area of north-eastern Belgium, where the battle was at its fiercest, was a mix of British and American forces with the latter priding itself by being the main majority The information had been spread, the war room plans exposed; it was 230,000 allied soldiers up against a jaw-dropping 405,000 Germans. They had to make every shot count.

Hayden was smoking a cigarette in the breeze, a glimpse of heat the only thing closest to a fire on the frontline. Things had to look real; they were ordered to be the cornerstone defence capable of holding of an entire German assault and could not be allowed to show their true, weakening numbers. Flint glanced up at the single Bren LMG sitting in position at the top of their foxhole, the barrel starting to create small icicles at the mouth. It had last been used a few weeks ago when the original counter-offensive into the forest towards the Rhine had been made. However, Flint was still recovering from being bombarded by his own planes back in the Bayeux fields to even have realised. After that firefight in the field and bombing runs, only a quarter of Delta Company had survived. More British reinforcements had arrived to the farmhouse and secured it, fortunately letting Bravo Six and the rest of the company relieved off their duties for the next couple of months. After those precious resting times, two more soldiers had joined Bravo Six in the early weeks of December. Then they were transported by truck to relieve the 101st American Airborne Division at Bastogne, an exhausted, outnumbered and starving small unit who had held off entire German battalions for the past weeks.

One of the new soldiers in Bravo Six was Scott Addington, a young classic Englishman who was a farmer and raised in Yorkshire. A very promising life lay ahead, to inherit their farm and have a free house from his retired father and mother. He had eight brothers (all of which had the same green eyes and cropped brown hair), whom of which were all dotted around the globe…France, North Africa, Italy, Taiwan – you name it they're there. His joyful life had ended when the war had erupted and spilled out of national control. All his country friends and brothers were split into different units, heavy in the navy and air force, however still, he preferred himself being in control of his life rather than letting man-made machinery, like a plane, decide his fate. Instead, he enlisted in the army. Strongly built, he was known well across his last platoon. Shame he had lost the whole lot.

Then there was Aaron White…the complete opposite. His life was for the city and grew up loving it. Having went to university at Cambridge, his personality mainly whirred around his humour and to make trouble. Typical. He was not the biggest man, being skinny and slim, but the black-haired twenty-year-old had an idea of how to fight. Both men were chatting in the closest foxhole to Flint's and covered themselves in fresh holly. Luckily, for Delta Company, they had been permitted leather gloves, a gift from the government. On the other hand, the Americans that came trudging towards the foxhole, with rifles slung over their backs, stood bare-handed.

"You boys know where Sergeant Brighton is?" the two Americans stated.

Flint took out his hand from beneath his frozen jacket and pointed a shaking, blue finger towards the foxhole ten metres away. One of the Americans nodded and walked over, their feet crunching in the snow. It was eight o'clock in the morning and the sun could just be seen shining through the cracks of the clouds and trees, rays melting through.

"It is freezing," mumbled Flint blankly with no expression on his face. Even though he had said it over a thousand times this morning, there was that little satisfaction repeating it again. Hayden looked up from the opposite side of the foxhole, his snowy helmet slanted to one side as tiny strands of blonde hair crept to his forehead. He had a white scarf wrapped around his neck and green collar. Flint recognised it. It was too cold to speak, but he said it anyway.

"Isn't that scarf from back at Sword?"

"Yeah, that boy by the bunkers. Figured I would need sometime during this war. Washed it a few weeks ago and looked brand-new. There's a card inside from his mother. It's German so I have no idea what it says." Hayden presented it slowly, a little snowflake rubbed onto it. It looked almost Victorian with the style engaged. Decorated clocks and a picture of a festive Dortmund. *It was the 23rd now, two days until Christmas*, Flint thought. He remembered his last Christmas. And how different it was! Last year he was having a glorious lunch with his father, brother and friends, eating a fresh turkey his father had bought with most of his spending money. There were crackers, music, huge tables for all the families loaded with warm food such as potatoes and gravy that he found delicious. Now he was sitting at the bottom of Belgium, without food, warmth and commanded to shoot anyone who wandered out from the opposite side of the forest.

Suddenly, a long, ear-splitting disturbance was followed by a huge thump. Flint, with on-point reaction from earlier conflicts, ducked and folded his hands over his helmet. Hayden did the same...then grinned as he glanced up...it wasn't German artillery, but a tree had frozen of its roots and tumbled onto Scott and Aaron's foxhole. Flint stood up and lifted himself out the hole, holding his M1 Garand as he paced over to the fallen spruce.

"That's just fantastic..." muttered Aaron as he tried to push the lengthy spruce tree of his chest. "Scott, tell me you're not hurt, man. I need to you to push this thing off."

Scott Addington smirked then heaved the tree off Aaron, his legs flinging in the snowy air as he was pinned.

"I'll help," announced Flint as he took the end of the spruce. Together, Flint and Scott lifted the tree off, chucking it into some bushes nearby.

Aaron stood up with his whole back in a smooth snow glaze…before he patted it off. Their foxhole was a complete shamble with mud and water filling it up; soaking everything inside.

"No, my chocolates are in there!" pointed Aaron as a single block lifted to the mucky surface. "You know how many rations it took to build that bar?"

Scott let out a quick laugh, sniggering as Flint and Hayden brushed the snow off their elbows.

"You can come into our foxhole, save you the trouble," Hayden exclaimed. He looked at Flint who slowly spread his cold hands into a thumbs-up.

"Yeah, thanks," Aaron replied. "We got an ammo box for you lot."

"Sure, put it under our Christmas tree!" remarked Flint.

They weaved around the trees back to Flint and Hayden's foxhole. Each group of soldiers were doing something different in their foxhole, smoking cigars mainly. Others were playing cards on wet pine blocks whilst some were looking at maps and tatty photographs of the Ardennes. None looked joyful to be here. The four Brits arrived at their foxhole, the snowflakes still raining from above. All climbed down into it and Scott placed the ammo box under their Christmas tree. It was an actual Christmas tree that Hayden had, by luck, found whilst wandering to the front lines. Little cigarette boxes acted like jingle bells and several were dotted all over, glimmering in the little bit of light there was. Aaron laughed.

"Hayden, I could definitely do with some of your herbs from back home!" Flint said and chuckled. Hayden sarcastically managed to pull a smile in disbelief.

"We're gonna need some of those on the night after the German's attack. Apparently, they've only got fifty men!" Scott smiled, as he knew the obvious odds of their defeat.

"But a new shipment of our own boys with field telephones are only getting supplied in tomorrow morning!" he grieved. Flint looked around at the hundred or so men in foxholes surrounding him, a deep murmur rinsing across. Hopefully, they could hold off fifty Germans!

"Tomorrow morning? What'd you say about that one, Flint?" Aaron sighed, sarcastically enthusiastic.

"Wait, so they moved us up but kept the radio guys hanging back? Bit stupid, that's what I think. Let's say we get attacked at dusk, how we meant to call for help?"

"They won't care," Hayden added on. "Bet Montgomery doesn't even realise he's got troops in Belgium."

"Well, he's apparently taken the whole of Africa already. Less fighting for us, I guess." Scott shrugged, still shaking as he slowly scrubbed the snow out from inside his boots.

"What I would trade to be in Egypt right now…by the Nile with my camels…" Aaron spelled out clearly. He chuckled to himself.

"Ah, well, at least we got some sun on our way here," Scott shared, his body warming to the thought.

"Oh, yeah? Where'd you go?" speculated Flint.

"Camped at Caen after we invaded it with the other half of the third. Luckily, they do have balconies that kept us occupied."

"How'd it go there, hard resistance? Me and my ex-battalion encountered some Germans in the cornfields near it, heard those AA guns at night, I tell you," Aaron insisted with wide eyes.

"We had eight thousand casualties all around." Scott looked at the ground. He then added with a hidden sorrow in his face, "Lost my whole squad. Every last one. My oldest brother, George, even joined the funeral list with 'em."

Flint and Hayden were both taken aback by the numbers and caught a glimpse of despair and hurt in Scott as he relayed the fallen memories over again.

"Where's the sergeant?" asked Aaron as he threw away the twigs from under his back, desperate to change the subject.

"I don't even know, though some yanks came and asked for him. Think he's probably with Lieutenant Cole," Hayden replied with a simple answer.

"Cole's back? I haven't seen the guy since Bayeux."

"What's that old man like? Brighton, was it?"

Flint and Hayden looked at each other as they realised the once-in-a-lifetime opportunity. Their smiles increasing whilst trying to find the right words.

"Brighton? He's actually really genuine, spared all his food for us back at Sword and a very, you know, 'loveable' guy. Softy," Flint exclaimed boldly, trying to persuade Aaron. He tried his hardest not to burst out laughing but yet still kept a dead straight face.

"Yeah, yeah, I agree with you, Flint. He's that one sergeant who is not a cold brick wall like Raymond, you know," Hayden added.

"Mind if I go and talk to him?" requested Aaron. "Might be good to make a first impression on the old man." He was clearly fooled and taken for a ride.

None of the four men felt the chilly ice of the December morning and were rather enjoying themselves now that they had company. Scott had realised the true nature of the profound sergeant and kept things to himself.

"Go ahead! Oh, and he hates the fact that people salute him. When he fought in…" an unsure hesitation followed, "…the Philippines, he lost all feeling in both arms; make sure you press hard when you give the man a hand-shake," both Hayden and Flint announced. Aaron, nodding, shrugged naively and staggered out of the foxhole, his M1 Garand wobbling as he got a foothold in the shrub and snow. The rest of the men wrapped themselves up in warmth once more, the wind starting to stir up once again through the bustle of the leaves. Flint waited until the sound of crunching feet had slowly faded then peered over the edge with the others.

"Aaron White's famous last day," murmured Flint, as the others laughed.

Aaron walked up to Sergeant Brighton who, perfectly timed, struck out from his foxhole. Brighton froze half-step. Not of the cold but because of the random soldier staring cluelessly at him. It was a few moments until Aaron's first movements emerged.

"Name's Private White, sir. Got disembarked from the 116th last week to join your platoon. I've heard a great deal about you, sir." Brighton pulled out a small smile in glee. The private added, "It's an honour."

Aaron approached the sergeant, the senior vividly noticing and patiently waiting for a brisk salute. It never came. The astonished sergeant glanced down before looking up, a glare of fire in his putrid eyes.

"What's the matter with you, private?" said Brighton as he witnessed the youthful man awaiting for a firm handshake. Aaron then retrieved, regretting his decision to introduce himself as he realised he had been slyly tricked.

SMACK!

A solid smack round the head steadily made contact with the back of Aaron's skull. He grunted then toppled to the floor. Flint, Scott and Hayden burst out laughing and rolled in their foxhole.

"Sorry, sir. The rest of the unit told me you…" mumbled Aaron as he gripped the left side of his face, slowly trying to disappear into the snow. He wished he could.

"Do you not know respect, private?"

Aaron blushed and felt mightily humiliated as he saw Cole peep his head out from over Brighton's shoulder in silence. He made a U-turn and walked back to his foxhole, ready and armed to give the rest of his platoon a verbal, maybe even physical, beating. Trudging through the cracked snow, he rolled over the events of how they persuaded him. He had seen the stiff smile from Scott as soon as he turned his back. How stupid he had been! It was such an easy one to commit to as well. Aaron clenched his bruised jaw and straightened his brown hair out properly. He looked towards the lonely forest in front where hundreds of American-British guns were aiming at.

Maybe it was just a severe lapse of poor judgement; concentration even. But unmistakably he heard the faint sounds of twigs snapping and the trees opposite caught in an almighty brushing noise. Something was there. And it did not look good.

The ultimately recognisable hood of a Nazi Tiger Tank emerged from the spruce trees and mounds of deep snow, camouflaged in an eerie pellucid white, which looked identical to the ground beneath its chugging wheels.

"Wh—"

BOOM!

Aaron opened his mouth to scream, to alert the others urgently. However, in a split-second he was trailing through the air at great speed, the earth on its axis. The renowned Tiger Tank had bolted a whizzing, deadly shell directly at him, only metres off from hitting the nail in the coffin. The allied soldiers smoking in the open suddenly noticed, leaping into random foxholes, not caring if they crushed one of their own but by caring for their own life. A chatter of machine gun fire ripped the roots of a tree next to Flint as Bravo Six scrambled for their weapons, searching for any anti-tank grenades or charges whilst they did so. Hayden peered over the edge of the foxhole and saw Aaron lying in the open, arms and legs wildly outstretched. He groaned to himself and dashed over to the downed new soldier fifteen metres away. Bullets, white and hot, flashed past him and collided with the trees as he heaved Aaron onto his shoulders, a desperate plead of mercy since the advancing German forces now had added more tanks to the offensive. Flint spotted some incoming infantry crawling into holes in the snow, and shot them before they could. Crimson red blood sprayed onto the snow.

"That's definitely a lot more than fifty!" Flint announced.

"Just get on the Bren!"

Flint heard Scott's cry and threw himself onto the LMG; feeling the cold and raw stinging of the chamber. With the feeling of power between his numb hands, he let the gun go wild, scattering immeasurable rounds into the dawning troops. The Germans came rushing in great numbers, surrounded by hundreds of trees and holes that were their only hope of cover. They were like ants storming out after the nest had fallen, alone and ragged. Flint took out who he could, slamming the bullets into them one by one. Dark holes ripped into their chests and arms, but before he knew it, the ammo had run out and the gun was left steaming bare dry. He yanked at the magazine, his body prepared for a clean loose take. But it never moved, the magazine was frozen solid. With the whistle and booming of the tank shells and orders of the men nearby, he barked for help, a short snap of twisted anger.

Hayden was still going. Trudging through the suffocating snow as bullets whizzed past, flicking bark of the trees beside him. Aaron was on his shoulders groaning in despair and left unconscious.

"Don't worry I got you, buddy!" Hayden exclaimed.

But he was done, even with the foxhole only metres away, his legs faded lame without consent, creating him to collapse onto a thick patch of vegetation, gulping down great lungful of air. His mouth seemed very damp despite the seemingly endless amount of solid snow around him. Finally, his senses re-emerged. Hayden looked up with a face full of leaves at Flint who was calling for help, oddly tugging at his stationary Bren. Scott's hands appeared and dragged Hayden into the foxhole, shrapnel just skimming his ankles as he did so. As he slid in, so did Aaron in a half-awake hurry. His eyes filled with quivering fear, which was quickly set alight by anger. Hayden noticed this and asked shortly:

"You all right?"

Aaron was still glaring forward, completely ignoring Hayden's heroic actions and he staggered to his feet with his sodden rifle. The Germans were getting closer, hundreds of them hiding behind burnt trees shaking with fear or shooting to rid their nerves. Aaron peered down the sights and snatched at the trigger. A German collapsed onto the floor as penetrating snaps of bullets whizzed into his head. Followed by another and another. Sergeant Raymond and the rest of Charlie Eight were perched in their foxhole behind Flint, carefully dotting pot-shots whilst searching for anti-tank machinery. They only had a stack of S.T Grenades. More commonly known as the Sticky Bomb.

Five more Tiger Tanks came rumbling in to support the charge. Defended and undeniably predatorial in attack, it is known as being one of the most advanced tanks of the time and completely obliterated most Shermans. It bore a ground-breaking 100mm thick frontal turret sheet of armour and a total weight of sixty-eight tons. It deemed fear into the allied hearts. Steadily coming in closer by the second, incoming rifle fire looked like miniature sparks at bonfire night.

"We're gonna need something a lot bigger!" howled Scott as a flick of lead slit across his helmet.

All four men in Flint's foxhole were suddenly blasted by a chain of bullets, slick and whistling. They lowered themselves and kept their heads down, looking on silently yet panicking at the oncoming onslaught of the machines.

Their hearts melted into doom and downcast.

An unexpected explosion erupted in the foxhole, sending Flint juddering to the side. The surviving soldiers of the blast came screeching out, horrified to see their friends they had just laughed with blown to bits. No more would they ever see each other. German soldiers had spotted them running and gunned them down in the open creating a domino-like effect on the men.

Flint lay against crumbling snow and dirt, stained in despair. But to his amazement, Sanders and Blackwell, from back at the farmhouse, suddenly emerged, crawling through the snow with faces twisted in dreaded anticipation. A glimpse of hope enlightened in the heart but the tank's engine got louder. Blackwell was holding an old, charred fabric bag jangling with numerous items inside.

"Where's the rest of Charlie Eight?" Flint asked upon sight. His helmet pinged off into some torn shrubs and he scooped it back on again. Sanders snatched and ripped open the bag, stick bombs spilling out.

"Back in the foxhole!" Sanders was barely able to hear himself under the gunfire and he carefully recollected the explosives. "We got stickies...on my count, cover me and I'll place these on the hood!"

Flint glanced at the last three Tiger Tanks, who were left, rolling on. The other pair were either currently set alight or in a ragged pile of iron impregnated with an intense clog of smoke ascending into the trees. Sanders signalled he was ready. A simple thumbs-up followed. His heart rapidly thudded until it actually hurt.

"Go!" Scott tossed his only smoke grenade into the air, the can popping open after a few precious seconds and unleashing a whirlwind of smoke. The tank had disappeared in the smoke, as well as its direct vision. Sanders grasped hold of the ripped roots stretching along the width of the foxhole and cautiously clambered his way out. Hayden, Blackwell, Aaron, Flint and Scott slotted their guns over the side, firing short bursts of accurate rifle fire to cover him. Now they had to keep him alive.

Flint crouched; his muddy hands shaking as he slowly pushed more bullets into the barren M1. He watched as the men behind him were doing their much needed bit too, bravely holding back the German forces whilst they brutally advanced.

CRACK!

A sudden snap and shriek were heard as Blackwell fell like a post backwards. A sniper had caught him through the head. He was dead before his cold body hit the bottom of the hole and the entire squad knew it. Flint wobbled back up again, hearing the whizzes of the bullets fly by his ears and pounding into the thick snow beside him. He fired multiple shots at two shattered Germans who came running on-fire through the smoke. What else was there!

Aaron was getting restless and constantly peered into the smoke to check on Sanders, who had not yet detonated or even placed the charges to his despair. But luckily, to their satisfaction, Bravo Six celebrated with cheers as an explosion rocked the earth around them. Where the booming sounds came from none cared, the tank was gone. Fire could be seen lingering above the smoke. It was a good sign.

"Ha ha!" Brighton could be heard laughing from the trees. Flint interrupted his delight and added to the reality.

"Well done, Sanders! You can come back now! Everyone, hold your fire, for a hero returns!"

But there were no sheets of metal scattering in the air or Germans stumbling out the flap of the vehicle. The cheering halted almost upon instant as the smoke slowly dissipated, revealing a much worse intended sight. The satchel was gone.

The sticky bombs nowhere to be seen. Like a knife to the heart, Flint spotted Sanders leg lying under a fresh coating of blackened ash. Looks as if he had been shot and killed with the satchel in-hand, creating a vigorous muffle of chained explosions.

"He's gone! We have nothing left!" Hayden and Aaron spat in fury.

"For what?" a hollering echo ascended from Lieutenant Cole a dozen metres back. "The Tiger's gone!"

Sergeant Raymond witnessed his dead comrade's limb exposed in plain sight. And as deeply saddened as he was, he sent the last platoon's man to the front foxhole with Bravo Six. His name was John Heaton, an experienced (nearly bald) veteran who fought a year earlier in the initial invasion of Sicily. Glorified for his distinctive acts in the south, he inherited the fact that he was one of the last British survivors to hold out to a huge German counter-attack at Ponte Grande. Heaton picked himself up and over cover, the only British soldier standing in the unprotected open, and – ran. *They probably need me now more than ever...*he whined to himself. A sudden intense hail of bullets came raining towards him, all in some unexplained way smashing into the bark beside him. Another pepper of shrapnel burst into the man near the foxhole behind him, completely flipping him backwards. Finally, with help of the bullet-riddled trees, he leaped down into Bravo Six's hole. Immediately, he noticed Blackwell's body staring lifelessly into the grey sky. Heaton saw the rest firing their rifles mercilessly at the opposing force, not even realising he was there. Aaron however bent down into the mud to reload and slipped into Blackwell's blood, his fingers twitching and turning a deep impenetrable shade of blue.

"Private White, I got more bombs for you!" Heaton reassured steadily as Aaron trudged towards him.

He thanked Heaton, checked the bag and called for Flint, who came with contagious hope on seeing the weapons in the fabric bag. Heaton carefully placed the sticky bombs to one side, minding sparks that might accidentally set it off and break open the whole allied line.

"Somebody's gonna have to take it," Aaron announced to the platoon. None answered.

"I got no smokes left," Scott muttered to himself, obviously annoyed.

Heaton added, "Who's gonna go then? We gonna pull straws?"

"I'll go."

Flint only realised seconds later what had just come out of his mouth. He had sentenced himself to a death. He never regretted it however; he would do it instead of the lives of his mates around him and for every man fighting for peace here.

The Bren LMG, sitting uselessly on the rim, finally defrosted enough and the magazine could just be slipped out. Scott loaded an entire new drum of ammunition into it and the gun was rearing to go on its bipod. With a barrel length of twenty-five inches and a rate of fire from 520 rounds per minute, it was known for taking out groups of riflemen dozens at a time.

"Flint, you good?" Hayden asked under the crackles of gunfire.

"Yeah. I'm gonna do it…yeah," he replied with a pant. Hayden thanked him and returned to his position on the right of the foxhole. Meanwhile, Heaton geared Flint up with the bombs and charges.

"Listen! There's no charge or fuse on these things…you're just gonna have to use your pistol to shoot them."

The three Tiger Tanks left were sitting ducks in the open, like statues, simply staying where they were as they bombarded the hidden British and Americans with shells. Flint made his way to the edge of the hole, increasingly queasy on his feet. Aaron patted him on the back, urging him to go before it was too late.

Flint's feet dragged him over the sides into a freezing, bitter whirlwind of snow and bullets. A bullet pinged past him and nearly took him off his feet; however, his courageous charge mounted and he solitary ran towards the steaming tank. He quickly stuck his hand in the bag. Taking out the prized weapon, he ducked as another shell came screaming at him. It had worked.

Flint had managed to free the living death zone and plant the mine, his hands trembling in fear as dozens of Nazis pointed and fired their rifles at him. From in his trouser pocket lay a simple handgun. He whipped it out gracefully, scattering the small bullets into the tank's hidden bomb…

BOOM!

A ridiculous shatter of scarlet coiled in front of Flint as the tank shimmered and slid to one side. The insides burned up however some lucky crewman had managed to bolt out into the wilderness, their own men accidentally firing on them. A cheer echoed behind Flint. He strode to the next tank, only metres away, the driver frantically turning to one side to allow the MG to fire. But it was too late once more. As tense and scared as he was, he darted and lay beneath the gun, which clogged and opened fire.

RATATATATA!

Flint felt the casings of the bullets drop onto him directly from above. They were like little pieces of melting metal, piercing his skin as he hid stone still. Despite the chaos around him, he still once more stuck the bomb on the steel armour plating, his fingers struggling to connect the wires. Once everything was in place, he slid into a nearby crater a metre away. The bullets flicked the snow centimetres from him, but Flint had a drastic plan.

He swiftly swerved the snow onto him, hoping no stray bullet nor metal casing would slit into his body. The snow was comforting, like a misleading lie dragging Flint in as his skin got significantly colder. A sudden vibration warped through the ground and he popped his head out, snow choking from his mouth as he slowly uncovered himself. His body was drenched. Wrapped in a layer of mental hypothermia. The second last Tiger Tank had finally exploded into a dazzle of light, the Brits in foxholes eager with anticipation as they kept the supressing fire on for Flint. But this time no live Germans came clambering out, for it was now a mixed mess of bent steel and iron.

One more to go.

"Go, Mitchell! We got you covered!"

Flint staggered to his feet and ran. He hadn't dare turn around whilst he struck towards the last tank, for a swift lack of concentration could endure a fate of perish in these Flemish woodlands. But he recognised that familiar voice. Sergeant Brighton along with Lieutenant Cole had come to help. Flint winded in and out of trees steadily, the very bark around him exploding into mist as chugs of dirt poured over him.

At first, the Germans were not angry nor hateful…but surprised, almost feeling as if this was a rogue reality! One lone British soldier had abandoned his whole company to run straight into enemy hands? *Forced P.O.W!* thought one German commander as he took his eyepatch off, thinking if this was some sort of dream. He was watching Flint intensely with a small yet elegant Luger P08 behind a tree. The unwelcoming sight of the barrel pinpointed on the fragile young male's head. But he dare not shoot to kill, for the boy's courage was to be honoured, enemy or not.

Therefore, upon this, he slowly slotted the gun back into his holster and turned the blind eye, literally. The commander's father had accomplished the same thing in Verdun at World War I...but had not made it out alive. He wished it wouldn't be the same for this Brit.

However, he then spotted the last stick bomb, which Flint carried further to his precious tanks. His mood changed drastically. Forgetting *all* the praise, he reached down for his holster. Suddenly, a snap and a twitch of severe pain rippled across his body as a single bullet sliced his finger off, crippling him down next to a freezing broken branch. He muttered fearful sayings in German and ordered for the best thing the allies would hear all day...

"Retreat! Retreat!" the crawling commander barked.

BANG!

Another shell rocketed into a foxhole far from Flint; however, the intense shrieks were still clearly heard. He was only five whole metres away now. Were the Germans finally going to end him?

He swiftly clambered up to the hood of mighty vehicle. The chime and stuttering of the wet engine inside didn't distract but encourage him to keep moving; stay wide-awake. *The people here to kill you are yards away*, he thought. Flint attached the last wire to the mainframe; hoping for a steady process. He slipped the sticky bomb onto the armour with a soft, satisfying click; like the popcorn back in forgotten London. A smile widened across the majority of his face as he saw the Germans pulling back; retreating into the frozen forest.

Someone put an end to that uplift. A wild but experienced German came roaring in with a bayonet, his body concealed behind the trees. A sickening and terrifying expression unravelled across his face. It was littered with deep scars and wounds. Flint had seen it coming but was too late to react, the cold pierce of the blade slit into his left shoulder, a fragrance of blood leaking onto the snow.

Both weren't going to give up. Flint still had his pistol wrapped up in his trousers, edging for use. But the old man had now realised it was there. His long brown beard was covered in icicles yet his vision was the last thing from affected...therefore sparking a ferocious hustle for the gun.

The old man pounded his fists into Flint. One after another. He then deeply growled, as if waiting for an instruction. Flint was petrified. With eyes wide open, he held his arms up for defence and returned with some solid uppercuts. But the man still pounced, grappling the shivering body of Flint onto the icy floor.

SMACK! SMACK! SMACK!

Flint was riddled with punches, his face bruising as the German's beastly eyes met with his. Dark with fury they were. He strained down for his holster despite the throbbing pain. The Tiger Tank was only two metres away now with chains of MG fire deluding their enemy.

There was no other choice.

He pointed the holster at the stick bomb and pulled the trigger. The pistol spat a small bullet, which cracked into the bomb, a juddering hit and shockwave created. Like a fiery wave, the flames and metal came striking down everywhere. Flint tried to crawl away and was finally let loose when the German on him was peppered with shrapnel in the back. A deep grunt muffled out the old man's mouth and he thudded to the snow. Flint covered his eyes as secondary explosions erupted inside the tank. More bits of razor metal came raining towards him. He used the German veteran as a protective shield.

The axis had failed. The whole mounting, superior attack on the few British defences went bust; they had not broken the chains of the 'Iron Wall' so they had called it. The casualties were high on both sides, racking up to the mid two hundreds for the Axis powers, but on the other hand, the exhausted and ammo-stripped defenders had only lost fifty, an outstanding victory which allowed a Sherman convoy and British Artillery units to make their way closer to the front. Even Bernard Montgomery, the head British general, had heard of the attack and respected his men's heroic efforts. But there was one German squad that had been captured and they begged for mercy like nothing before.

"You ain't going nowhere, you pig," spat Brighton as he shackled a metal chain around one of the prisoners.

Hayden ran over to Flint, finding him half-submerged in the snow with a dead soldier on him. Flint shook his head, happy to see his best friend still alive. With a hand up, both trudged over to the rounded P.O.Ws who were handing their weapons in, one of them looking particularly dismal.

"Word has it if they did this to us, we would be in camps right now," Hayden muttered to Flint. Flint sighed and felt happy that wasn't the result.

"All the reason to kill 'em," Brighton interrupted as he shoved his way through. Hayden tried to tug his arm back but let go. Brighton pivoted back and gave him a sick glare. He took out his pistol, the barrel lying softly on the kneeling German's head.

"Nein! Errrr…er…" the German scrambled for the right English words, his body shaking in fear. Brighton's hand crunched harder on the base of the gun. His veins visible and filled with hateful blood. The man squirmed distinctively.

"Hey, don't do it. We're not one of them."

It was Flint himself who spoke up, prepared to be humiliated by the looming sergeant.

"'Course I'm not gonna do it…just shows you, though, how caring you are to the people that have come to kill you," Brighton whispered – it was more of a hiss than a whisper. Like a lurking dragon in a cave. The whole situation had reminded of previous fighting in Burma and it sliced a deep margin in his life. He didn't want to replay it. For a moment, Flint thought he had showed mercy. For once! "Cole, just get this guy in the truck."

It was the first time Flint had heard Lieutenant Cole speak in a respectful tone since Bayeux. His injury to the neck and recovery in hospital meant he had only regrouped with them in recent days.

"Yes, sir." He nodded and tucked his pistol into his back pocket cleanly. "All right all you Deutschman, file up!"

The remaining Germans were thrown onto ground, before being yanked back up and chucked mercilessly into the boot of the trucks.

"Never surrender!" a tangled German roared.

He took out a hidden MP40 from under his burnt jacket and triple-shot his own German commander next to him in the chest, doing this while shrieking the words:

"Traitors! Cowards!"

He then shot another young German next to him before obliterated as the staggered Brits opened fire. The bullets zipped in and out of him, even with his body falling over and lying flat on the ground. The British only stopped firing ten seconds after he had dropped. One last German stood statue-like still, the only man to be so still that not even his jacket's edges would flutter in the soft winds.

Shaking with fury, Sergeant Brighton took out his pistol once again, smacking the butt of it into the prisoner's chin. The 'enemy' did nothing in retaliation, only crashing into the floor, and slumping next to a patch of sodden shrubs with his back against a tree. He had just witnessed his whole squad gone in a minute and whined helplessly as the British sergeant pointed the gun at him once more.

"*Bitte, bitte!*" the German sobbed. 'Please, please!' was the message.

"What was that?" Brighton put his hand behind his ear and listened.

He knew what it meant. He understood German fluently and used the opportunity to show no pity on the man. For Flint? He had enough. The careless and cruel acts of his comrades had driven the respect well out. It showed that the allies were not always as good as the world portrays them as; instead, a small handful like Brighton were crammed with vicious and vile behaviour.

Flint smacked the gun out of the sergeant's hand and threw it to the side. Brighton reacted with a shove; a sense of surprise mixed in, and felt gobsmacked that his own man would dare come up to him. He loomed over Flint, stalking right up to his face. Flint knew he was bigger, taller and probably stronger. But he didn't care. What he was doing was wrong.

Hayden came and split his way in the middle, trying to stop the argument. Brighton slung Hayden to one side, toppling into the snow. He then did the same to Flint, but there was more resistance, a tight position that took Brighton some strength to throw him over. Aaron and Scott dashed over from the foxholes with weary faces scrubbed in mud and blood.

"Stop now, okay!" Aaron barked as he helped pick Hayden up, his backpack weighing him down.

"These are the people who massacre schools and bomb cities!" roared Brighton.

"We don't know about him!" Flint panted. "He could've just signed up!"

"He's still one of them! Don't you get it? After one, there's another! Each believing he can be like the last man!"

Flint wobbled to his feet with aching legs and a bleeding nose; however, Brighton smacked him back down with an elbow to the jaw.

"How'd you like that, huh? Huh? Tell me?" muttered Brighton at Flint who was dragging himself off the ground.

"Much better," spat Flint.

The two stared at one another.

BANG!

Brighton glanced at his pistol in his holster, wondering if it had accidentally misfired. The standing German cried in agony and lumbered back onto his face. His empty body thumped onto the cold earth. A pool of blood seeped around him and his eyes gazed lifelessly open. The cause from a gaping hole sitting in his chest.

"Score!" Sergeant Raymond said and chuckled as he pumped the second shell into his Winchester M12 shotgun. The huddle gathered around him let out a few chuckles. He then added with a smirk whilst intentionally staring at Flint and Hayden, "Got 'em!"

Flint didn't react. Neither did Hayden.

"What's wrong with him?"

"He's from one of the older units, fought at Norway before he came."

"Back to your foxholes, men," commanded Brighton, interrupting Hayden, as he wiped the blood off his sleeve. "We're moving out," he added with a sinister hiss into Flint's face.

12 – Chills of Dusk

The companies who fended off the German offensive stalked through the ever-growing woodland; swallowed up into the mist of spruce trees and pellucid snow. Low on sleep but refreshed on ammo, they strode through, highly eager to rid themselves of the entangled wastelands of Flemish vegetation. Every step was a risk. The occasional Nazi sniper in pure white would be discovered roaming the terrain; spying on weary legions of allied soldiers that came wandering across these icy paths. Delta Company had managed to locate a whole burrow of them. Each one frozen into the ground having being lost in the widespread of the forest. Flint Mitchell had no mercy for them, despite willing to defend regular soldier's lives when captured. For him these were unseen creatures, killing not in the heat of battle but in the downfall of nowhere. It was his biggest phobia. The whole platoon felt it in the chilling breeze too.

"You guys okay back there?" Flint questioned as he leaned back to Aaron and Scott. Their feet crunched on the snow and they let their rifles loosely sway in their hands.

"Well, apart from all this" – Aaron took off his helmet and bashed it against his M1 Garand; handfuls of snow fell out – "I think we're good."

Scott, a face perplexed in the homesickness most young men engulfed, nodded and asked, "How long 'til the end of this forest, Hayden?"

"Don't know…probably couple dozen miles or so," Hayden replied unsatisfactorily. Flint pondered and took out his map, blowing the snow off.

"Sergeant gave this to me. Some American dropped it by one of the burning tanks."

"Well done, yank," Aaron commented.

Flint studied the map whilst marching, searching for where they were. It was extremely challenging to navigate in this dense forest. He couldn't find them anywhere in the broad map!

"Well, I can't see us, but I guess we're along this path here." Flint showed the others and pointed his shaking finger at a small opening quite close to a nearby river.

"Yeah, probably…is that the Rhine though?" Aaron signalled at a long strip of water winding a few miles through wastelands. Hayden tried to answer briefly with a tone of irritancy. *What else could it be!* He moaned to himself. The fighting and lack of sleep was slowly rooting into him.

Flint, noticing the deprivation, answered for him, "Yep. One of the last bridges standing across it is located just a few kilometres from here. The Germans has completely locked it down. Most likely rigged it with a whole lotta dynamite."

"How we gonna get across it then?" moaned Scott. "I'm not swimming in water at minus twenty!"

"Depends. Probably by storming from the front but that's probably not such a good idea. Ask Lieutenant, he'll know," replied Flint whilst looking at the overcast sky above. He heard the sudden growing noise of feet crunching across the snow. Heaton came walking towards them, a woolly green beanie across his head.

"Operation Plunder," he blurted out. He then coughed a few times before sneezing. "Think that's what you're trying to say."

Flint and the others nodded when they realised. He chuckled to himself and advanced closer to the steadily walking squad, seeing the two leaders up front split from the rest.

"That the name for the Rhine offensive?" Hayden asked blankly. Heaton did a numb thumbs-up.

"Oh, and also we're close to Germany," he mumbled.

"Yeah? How far?" Flint smiled as he said this, knowing they were nowhere near.

Scott countered swiftly, "Guess what's waiting there for us. Another whole country of machine gunners, that's what."

"Not far off," remarked Flint.

"Oi. Keeps your voices down, will you? Snipers are prowling these areas like wolves," Brighton declared coldly without looking back. The others shrugged. The sergeant replied, "I mean carry on if you want to be lying dead next to a tree trunk."

"You heard him," Cole announced after a brief pause. "They're everywhere."

Aaron was about to talk once more when Brighton's intercom blared out, the crackling distinctively heard. A deep yet modest voice awaited them.

"Bravo Six and Charlie Eight, this is Staff Sergeant J.T Edwards from 00GY9-TL, we've located a possible German weapons refinery ten kilometres east of your position. Over."

"Copy. What do you want us to do, sir?"
Flint listened in more closely like everyone else, wanting to know where their next possible deathbed would be...

"Orders from Montgomery's 21st Army Group state that you attack at first light tomorrow whilst being escorted by the rest of the British 3rd Division; who are currently based at Caen. No to light resistance predicted. Meet at co-ordinates SD-F31286 at 07:00 and get in the jeeps with the third."

"What 'bout the Ardennes?" muttered Brighton.

"The Ardennes?" The radioman could be heard having a muffled chuckle. *"Don't worry about that...we got 500,000 men on the job. This is your new assignment. Oh, and it's your last solo mission Bravo Six, so be happy. After this, it's the Rhine...then you're all going home. Good luck."*

"Will do. Over and out," Brighton said and coughed.
Silence returned.
Flint breathed out a deep gulp of air and watched as it dissipated into the trees...thinking about the times that led him here. His dad and Christopher were still clocking in his head even though it felt like a century since...or more. His mother too. The others, however, were thinking about the upcoming mission that they had been specially granted with.

"That guy's definitely from Manchester," remarked Aaron with a chuckle from Hayden and Heaton.

"You hear that, lads? Last solo mission," Cole pronounced in an uplifting tone. Heaton suddenly remembered about his own platoon and ran to them to tell the good news.

"Yeah. It feels good I'll tell ya," Scott stuttered and started walking along the frozen path again.

Brighton crouched down and searched briefly in his backpack, his lips moving in silence yet nothing coming out. He then recalled, "Ah, Flint, pass the map. Would you?" Flint handed it over quickly and the sergeant studied it. "The refinery is only an hour and a half from here. We'll stay the night camped at this spot, create a perimeter."

"Wait, Sergeant?" Flint stuttered as he walked over to Brighton who picked damp and wet logs off the floor for a fire. "Isn't the initial crossings of the Rhine only in March?"

Brighton looked at him whilst throwing a maggot-infested twig to some evergreen bushes.

"The Americans and most of our army attack then. For us? When we get to the Rhine River, they're just using us to test their defences. What else would we be doing?" he responded sourly and still edged over the brawl they had. Flint was shocked upon answer.

"So we're like…dummies?"

Brighton flickered the falling snow from his eyes and responded ungracefully, "You heard me."

For the next quarter-hour, Flint searched for dry firewood propped up against a shelter-like area where no snow could split through. It was hopeless. The stuff was everywhere! But with the support of the rest of the group, they managed to scrape up a few hefty logs to keep them going through the night. Charlie Eight on the other hand had nicked some blazing wood and created their own. Before long, a fire ignited and the group settled down near the flames, wanting a touch and splendour of heat.

Flint and Hayden watched the crackles and yellow embers illuminate themselves, the orange flames licking at the air. It danced, almost as if it was living, the changing colours from red to yellow to blue giving it the appearance of a glorious sunset. It seemed quite the opposite of how the squad was feeling now…

As Flint lay against the fallen tree trunks with stones pre-laid beneath him, the light of the forest began to mystically fade. The shimmers and rays of light had been concealed in a dark union of night. The wind wailed against the tree hollows and distorted trees. A more negative approach to the wilderness had just arrived as everything visible melted into the invisible. Goosebumps eerily crawled through Flint's spine as he tried to set himself to sleep. He could not do it even with the doubtful certainty of how hard he tried! Just in case of an ambush, he kept his M1 Garand near him for safe keepings. *Who would even want to attack in this weather?* he thought. His top bid was most indefinitely the Japanese. The bare branches above him spiked into the moon's shimmers of light – no source of heat except from the deteriorating fire that quenched to its last flames. The cold whistle of the trees finally ended as the night descended into a calm yet eerily silent mood…

13 – Burnout

ey, Flint...wake up.

He opened his eyes despite the energy-lacking strain on them and the sudden calling. Flint spotted Scott and Hayden over to his right, shivering whilst stamping out the remains of the sodden fire logs. Brighton and Cole lingered on the left, studying the map and scribbling pencil markings all over it, desperate to get out the cold winter's morning. He felt his muscles ache and tense up as he slowly grabbed onto Aaron's outstretched helping hand. The very life had been hit out of him as he grasped to his feet, peering around him at the decaying trees and the usual white blanket of snow. Aaron passed over his M1 Garand and helmet and Flint slotted both on lazily, 'ready' for another day in which he would most likely get killed. As he punched the final rounds of bullets into the magazine, Lieutenant Cole wandered over to him rubbing his chin.

"You okay, Mitchell?"

"Ha. Never felt better, sir!" Flint just managed to grin – painfully.

He glanced at the two left in Charlie Eight, Sergeants Raymond and Heaton, who both were stacking ammo into their jackets.

Cole patted him on the shoulder and the squad set off once more through the harsh forest, feet slogging and hands blue from the environment. They steadily walked in a dense pack across the remaining terrain of the Ardennes; hoping for more than just suffering alone. The route to the rally point for the waiting 3rd Division was relatively simple; a long walk past the seemingly endless hedgerows and a sharp left to a little dirt road. Flint arrived in no time, his limbs hurting from the various explosions yesterday and the feeling for the will to fight had completely and utterly dispersed.

"I think that's the rest of 'em!" alerted Hayden. He had spotted a winding convoy driving over broken trees with union jacks imprinted on the sides; the engines heard wheezing on low diesel. It had to be the third division. Flint jogged over to his friend and peered over a tree stump edging closer to the gather of trucks twenty metres away.

"That's them all right!" Brighton called in a deep voice and lowered down his rifle, making his way down the hill towards them. "Come on the rest of you."

The jeeps halted and a single door swung wide open.

"Sergeant Brighton?" a short skinny soldier questioned as he clambered out – Brighton nodded. "British 3rd Division, you're coming with us."

They all loaded into the back of the jeeps, surrounded by multiple men from the same division.

The man sitting opposite Flint had his muddy helmet lopsided; a patched wound on the side of his head covered the burnt hair. The jangle of his ammo chain for his Sten submachine gun rang in the jeep and clanged with his tied belt. The men were gloomy, emotions ripped out and scavenged by the violence of the fighting in Caen. Most looked down at the floor of the moving and bumping jeep, staring lifelessly into the tiny dirt particles that lay collecting dust in the corner. The men's faces were like downcast statues, not even one flicker of movement. It reminded Flint of Brighton sometimes. He also wondered if Bravo Six appeared the same…

"What's happened to your engine?" Aaron asked as the constant wheezing noise echoed every time the tire turned. "Had to use a spare?"

Their lieutenant, Peter Ash, looked up from fixing his Lee-Enfield and watched the forest wade away from out the jeep. He mustered up the energy to speak. "On our way to come and get you guys, some sniper shot at the oil filter. For the past hour that piece of lead has been stuck in there."

This sparked a laugh from the men in the jeep and a conversation gradually swayed.

Finally, after an hour and a half of driving through Belgium wastelands and white corn plains, they arrived at the refinery. It was a deep complex of metal and rusting iron. Vine entanglements were common throughout the sector and doomed the grey, twisting structures to a suffocating end. Four airplane hangar-like buildings stood isolated in the open in a square perimeter. They were named the 'storages' as they stored anything such as oil drums or spare bits of axis machinery. A clear path of brick roads slicked through the entire complex, and at the end, glazed two large pale pillars filled with gallons upon gallons of darkening petroleum and water. The forest loomed behind and outlined the edges in a rectangle perimeter. Potholes and ditches greeted them as they leaped off the jeeps, rallying up in the woods to begin the operation. Around twenty-five men used this opportunity to huddle around inside a large crater in the depth of the forest; a dozen yards from the security perimeter of the refinery.

"Okay, listen up," whispered Sergeant Raymond who crouched down, shaking with fearful adrenaline. They all turned their attention to him as he began to talk. "This refinery is the only thing aiding the Germans in this sector...it's stopped our advance to the Rhine and to Germany. If we take it, our fellow men and Americans have a free passage through. If we don't, hundreds of more lives will be wasted for achieving a simple task. This is it. Seek and destroy. No one makes a sound on my command. Sound good?"

The soldiers and Flint responded quietly in agreement, willing to get started so that their pounding fears could drown.

"Then let's move out..."

Brighton came to the front and explained one last thing whilst gleefully loading his M1911 pistol.

"They got around thirty here apparently, so make every shot count will you?"

"Sure thing, Sergeant. Just make sure to do it yourself?" imitated Aaron who looked down quickly at the icy floor as Brighton whipped his head around. Both said nothing.

"One more thing," he hissed quietly with menacing eyes darting at Flint, "taking the refinery is top priority; prisoners are second. Don't get the two mixed up and *definitely* do not instantly resort to the second. Let's move."

All twenty-five men swiftly sped around the trees, heading down a slight hill. Flint hadn't even realised his hands were shaking as he ran through the last stretch of woods. They were numb, blue and inherited sudden reactions to a pre-firefight. He had to relax...but how could he! *Just stick to the mission, it will see you through,* he remembered Brighton's words before D-Day as they came up to the tree line, fifteen metres from the first storage building. If he could survive invading a machine gun beach with no cover, surely he could do the same for a simple refinery.

"Now," muttered Brighton.

Sergeant Raymond was first out the concealed bushes and into the light, his path followed bravely by soldiers. The sunlight rays illuminated their uniforms in the light however quickly descended as they propped up into defensive positions upon contact. He was out in the grass in a hurry but with luck, swiftly found suitable cover in a matter of metres, joyful to no longer be in the clear. The rest rushed up to the metal exterior wall of the storage unit. Iron sheets were stacked surrounding them and rusting in a deep glaze of orange-brown. It looked abandoned. It should've been. Hayden piled up next to Flint wishing he were back in England rather than this dump.

"Where the guards at?" he whispered whilst panting from the hinted adrenaline. Flint was too concentrated on looking around him for any enemy movement. The odd shadow or something that seemed remotely out of touch slammed Flint into the instant mode of aiming down the sights of his rifle. Brighton signalled to 'advance' with his hands and slowly ducked beneath a slow leaking oil barrel. The main pillars were twenty metres opposite them, huge poles of white, and the other storage containments on his right. Flint held his helmet and let the rifle swing in one hand as he dashed forward inside the first hangar-like area. Aaron nervously followed and then Scott. The wind gushed in through the cracks in the ceiling three metres above and slowly settled inside to a chilling mute…

"Heaton," Sergeant Raymond snapped quietly, "get over here, I need you with me."

Heaton nodded and bolted to his sergeant who lay propped up against a fallen lamppost. Flint saw the very sweat drip off his forehead and saw a figure radiated in the darkness, looming closer. He hissed quietly, "Get down! Guards!"

All men dropped their heads behind cover in seconds and locked their weapons.

The man still kept in the dark, his silhouette the only hint of where he shifted…

"Move."

Like a slowly turning wave, the third division crept up on the unseen German guard like forgotten shadows lurking in the corners, awaiting one to step near. Their luck a reverse repel.

A solitary guard dressed in a black and red SS uniform, strolled down the middle sector of the storage and his face was revealed in the cracks of shimmering light. He untied the metal wire locking the door and slowly heaved the back gate open, creaking as it did so. He inherited deep black eyebrows and pale skin, his hair was neatly folded under his Nazi cap and he looked as if to be somehow enjoying himself whilst inspecting his MP40. The British crouched perfectly still in the darkness of shadows and behind oil barrels, desperate for the lone soldier not to see them. Flint slowly lifted his foot the tiniest fraction to reach for his knife.

CRASH!

A box of rusty nails fell of an oil barrel next to Flint's feet and cascaded to the floor, shattering as they rolled towards him one by one. Flint closed his eyes tightly and couldn't believe what had just happened! He had just doomed his whole platoon. The perplexed SS member gazed at Flint's area, a face of uncertainty mixed with an unshakeable wall of no-fear as he stood with a high chest, marching towards the nails. He was humming an original orchestra piece from Germany and was clearly enjoying it as he bounded in closer for the kill…
A grim smile crossed his face…

CRASH!

The SS soldier was only two metres away from the crouching Flint when a stack of damp, rotten wooden planks fell from the wall behind him. Surprised and sensing the feeling of growing unrest, Flint carefully peeped over the edge and spotted Hayden; alerting the squad, he had knocked over the planks as a distraction for Flint. The SS man turned around and raised his sub-machine gun towards it.
Flint struck.
He leaped over the barrel and ran at the guard, growling as he did so. The guard turned around at the last second and felt a mighty punch throw him sideways to the floor. His MP40 slid to a halt and banged into a barrel. The German tried to defend himself by swinging random arms in the air hopelessly. Flint jumped onto him, battering him with his fists…then finishing him off with his knife in a clearly brutal fashion.
"Mitchell? You good?" asked Brighton as he crept up behind him. Flint nodded and wiped his blood-stained hands on his trousers. Brighton smiled. "You're a natural."
Ignoring the witty remark, Flint stood back up and whispered, "Sergeant…I think some of us should head left and not all group together. Germans gonna take a lotta lives with your strategy."

Brighton cluelessly stared at him for a few seconds before replying, "You want to live, Private Mitchell?"

"Very much, sir."

"Then shut up and follow my orders," Brighton coldly snapped.

"Move!" called Raymond as he dashed back outside to the centre of the complex. The rest followed once more with Bravo Six tagging at the back. They staggered into the light and looked around, surrounded by watchtowers with unlit spotlights. Raymond advanced deeper. The line of soldiers hid in the first storage unit whilst the sergeants prepared a plan of action from what they could see. Everyone kept a precise eye out for more hidden guards. Every window, locked door, open door, ceiling and pothole was a potential threat.

"Mitchell, White, Hendrix, Addington get over here," commanded Brighton quietly. The four rushed out from cover and to Brighton who sat behind a high stack of chopped oak. "All of you, go to the second refinery and secure the area; don't let anyone make a noise until we say so. If you do encounter Germans though, don't hesitate to light 'em up. You'll have to go through the office block first. Mitchell, you lead. Go!"

Flint nodded and wiped his forehead nervously. He did not like the sound of him being the first man in, but he would do it instead of his friends. Maybe it was a cruel revenge tactic brought up by Brighton, but he fathomed the idea. Hayden, Scott and Aaron followed closely as Flint winded in and out the storage unit, heading into a basic medium-sized brick office building. Flint held up his hand as they ascended to the main entrance. A simple rotten wooden door crawling with ivy. All halted.

"Left side door breach…stack up."

The squad lined up to the side of the door, waiting patiently for Flint's next order.

"Scott, take point," whispered Flint as he tried to unlock the locked door, it wouldn't budge. The door had stopped them in their tracks and to make matters worse, miniature voices could be heard discretely inside.

"*Ich denke…die Britisch sind hier…*" a muffled quiver echoed from inside.

"Don't worry, I got this…" Scott muttered. Hayden's eyebrows narrowed and discussed his thought.

"Sergeant said to make no sound, Scott."

Private Addington glanced up halfway from walking up to the door.

"How we gonna breach quietly? It's us or them."

He pulled out his personal shotgun from Caen, engravings of his fallen comrades' initials across the strap. It was a Winchester Model 1897 (also known as the Trench Gun) and was a heavy, pump-action one-barrel shotgun that he kept for 'special occasions'. A deep dark shade of acacia brown had been glazed over it and it looked significantly different from Sergeant Raymond's M12 variant. Bravo Six waited for Scott to make his way to the entrance.

BANG! BANG! BANG!

Scott blasted all three hinges off the door and kicked it down, shatters of wood and plant spraying in and out. The door tumbled down and revealed a couple of German soldiers smoking and reading magazines.

"Nein!"

"Die Nazi scum."

BANG! BANG!

The Germans were thrown across the pellet-ridden corridor in a bloody mess of bullets and cigars; their bodies lay sprawled awkwardly on the soaked beige carpet. No screams were heard and Scott smirked whilst pumping his Winchester once more, glad to have owned two so quickly.

"Go," he quietly pronounced.

"Nice shootin', mate. Real quiet," Hayden sarcastically complimented as he patted him on the back.

Flint, Hayden and Aaron rushed in; disgusted by the amount of blood that had been splattered across the walls. It had reminded of him of how his late uncle had died. Cold-heartedly killed in vain.

"You get used to it," Scott whispered as he joined the back of the line upon noticing the facial expressions. Flint approached two rooms, one right, one left at the end of the corridor. Simple offices yet deserted and empty in life greeted him from both sides. A single chair lay across the floor surrounded by mouldy rose paintings on the walls.

"Clear!" called Aaron from the other room.

"Clear here too!" Scott echoed through the corridor.

Flint peered at the separate art pieces, a spark of hope and faint remedies of his once normal life. He turned back around, feeling the coldness of the rifle in hands and ordered, "Good. Let's make our way to the second refer—"

RATATATA!

Suddenly, a rip of machine gun bullets split through the walls and tore the paintings to shreds, leaving them to crash to the ground. The brick walls brutally exploded from the silence as a chain of bullets zipped into the corridor. The lead sprayed across the width of the building and Bravo Six threw themselves to the smoking carpet. Hayden was so intensely surprised that he just stood there for a moment. Almost paralysed.

RATATATA!

"Get down!" cried Flint.

"Where's it coming from!" Scott screamed angrily.

The walls and carpets ripped open around Flint, flinging books and tables onto him. Hayden leapt down and crawled back towards the entrance, feeling the very bullets skim his ear, red and hot, as he waddled past the doorway. Aaron let out a shriek and ran into the next room of the first floor, a small kitchen area with a dirty window and balcony. More bullets split through the torn walls, encouraging Flint to get out of there, and get out the way. Quick.

Sergeant Brighton heard the lightning bullets crack into the offices and ordered a full-out attack, wanting to relieve the pressure his squad were violently soaking up. The twenty men dashed into the open once again, most clinging their green helmets whilst looking for the enemy. Heaton suddenly spotted the Germans lying with blasting MG42s in the windows on the office block opposite to Flint's. They looked like they didn't even care what they were doing!

Aaron glanced at the balcony and hit himself, annoyed that this was the only option out. The bullets whizzing into his room were increasing by the second. Ricocheting into the rusting oven and empty sink before pounding outside.

He jumped.

"Germans in the building on the right! Friendlies on the left! Move!" Heaton shrieked.

Brighton crouched behind a wheel barrel and lifted his rifle up towards the windows on the second floor. He saw the white of their eyes and shot.

"Help!" one German screamed hopelessly.

He crashed out of the building's window and smacked onto the floor ten metres below. The glass showered nearby Brits and sent them falling to the ground, their blood spraying in the air as they were gunned down by more hidden Germans.

"Grenade!" shouted a British soldier as he tossed a single frag through the window. The shooting and flashes were replaced by ear-piercing wails.

BANG!

A cloud of flames and dust erupted from inside the building. Bricks smashed out the window and smacked into the floor. Coughing and spluttering was heard as the Germans tried to escape however, they were helplessly caved in by a wall of fire, unshakeable to human force. The second floor shook and Germans came raining out, flying in the air and landing onto the cobblestone, their faces wild with dreaded fear and agonising pain. Either on fire or not, the British kept shooting them, forgetting the idea they had no weapons. The crawling bodies littered the floor and pools of blood were soaked across them.

The sheer amount of them downed looked like a quick victory however, the hidden Germans with Sturmgewehr 44s behind the refinery told another story. While Brighton fired several shots at a German behind another window, he heard a crunching sound and a thud directly behind. He reloaded his rifle and spun around.

It was Aaron.

He was lying dead still on the pavement with bruises and cuts scattered along his face.

Dead still.

He had just jumped out of the first floor window, which now suddenly erupted into a ball of flames, debris clanging onto the floor below. Brighton looked for a head wound, and found a small gash, before dragging him behind a rusting metal face, bronze in colour. He swiped out his canteen of water and took Aaron's muddy helmet off, sprinkling the rations onto his wounds.

"Come on, White," Brighton encouraged as he wrapped a wet bandage around his head and hair. Blood began to seep through. It dripped onto the floor next to him, slowly spilling off into a stream down into a nearby drain. Things were not looking good. At all.

Meanwhile, Flint, Scott and Hayden were having troubles of their own. The walls had been so damaged that they began to crumble, spitting out bricks into the centre of the rooms.

"Hayden…Hayden! Where are you?" shrieked Flint with a mouth full of concrete. A short reply was heard.

"Over here!"

Flint heard it and dashed into the corridor, speeding down the stairs five steps at a time and strapping the M1 Garand across his shoulders. He saw Hayden for a split-second, trying to run towards the entrance door, his face covered in ash.

"Oh, Flint!" he cheered. Flint leaped over the dead German bodies from earlier and sprinted towards him. The very cracks of the ceiling above could be heard and tears of brick and metal split through the floor.

"Get out!" Flint's scream echoed. Another yet different deep, thunderous rip was heard and Hayden stopped, looking up at the hole in the ceiling.

"Fli—"

An avalanche of brick and debris cascaded onto Hayden, a distinct cry heard as he slipped away into the rumbling fog. Flint heard his body smash to the ground, piled on by hundreds of brick that seemingly never stopped raining down.

"No!" Flint said sobbing.

He had no time for mourning and ran back towards the room he originally came from. It looked incredibly different from when he first entered it. The walls were cracked and smothered in bullet-holes and the floor blanketed in shredded tables and bricks. He had no time to investigate and before he knew it, he was smashing into the fire exit and into the outside world. The wind breezed gently on his face, as he looked back, the whole building crumbled to a mighty pile of snapped metal poles and bricks. Hayden was gone.

Luckily, he still had his helmet on…however for his pistol and canteen? Both were probably broken in the middle of debris metres away. He searched around for him; looking for any British servicemen under the stones. He could still hear the cracks of gunfire and booming of grenades near him, the occasional yet 'known-to-well' calls for a medic also greeted him. And that was when he heard Aaron's voice. It was moaning, like a poached rhino…stranded. He turned the refinery corner and saw him lying outstretched on the bloody pavement with

Brighton aiding him. Both looked scarce and pale. He couldn't lose three in one day!

"Aaron!" he yelled as he limped towards the casualty. Brighton looked up with weary eyes, the scar on his neck beating with dread.

"I've strapped up his gash on the head. See if there's anything else, I have no idea where all this blood is coming from!" Brighton exclaimed as he revealed his red-stained hands.

The pair, however, failed to realise that they were like sitting ducks, crouching in the middle of the pavement with too many upmost worries. A dozen German assault troopers, behind the first refinery, aimed down their iron sights on the sergeant and the young man with no rifle. They let the crippled, injured, one be. He was going to die of blood loss in a minute or so anyway. From twenty metres away, the men pulled the trigger.

RATATATATA!

The German Sturmgewehrs scattered a hail of bullets at the trio, the gun literally rattling in their hands as they struggled to maintain stable control. Brighton screamed as a bullet skimmed his cheek, stripping skin off into the pavement. A fragment smacked into Flint's rifle and flung it to the side. Not concentrating, he dragged Aaron across the road and behind the rubble with legs running horrifically fast. Another single bullet pinged his helmet off in the middle of the road…making it spin on its axis. The lead slapped onto the road around them with fury, chucking up pockets of concrete that created a heavy mist of surrounding dust. Flint made it and lay against a wall of rubble, happy with the safety around them – but panting as more bullets whizzed over their heads.

"Help! Help!" bellowed Brighton whilst lining up shots against the attackers. A squad of British soldiers came running towards them with faces twisted in grit. As always, some of them never made it, crippling to the floor by bullets that ripped over Flint's head. A duo .50 Cal team prepped their gun up against a mound of dirt, desperate to not get killed whilst doing it. One soldier fed in belts of cold ammo and alerted the other to fire…

"It's good t' go!"

Mini explosions rocked the earth around the Germans. They were pounded by round after round of bullets that pierced the refinery, spilling all the contents, which drifted slowly to the enemy soldiers' shoes. A spark flared off suddenly and chain reaction of wild fire began. The hidden Germans tumbled to the floor in a ball of molten flames.

"Sergeant! Pass Aaron's rifle!" Flint signalled. He took Aaron's Lee-Enfield from out of Brighton's hand and scoped down the sights.

KWA! KWA! KWA!

The bolt-action rifle had a different noise than the M1 Garand, a more silky, smoother taste to it. But that definitely didn't make it less deadly. Flint carefully whipped the Germans down with clean shots to the head and heart. *Sure,* he thought, *it wasn't the most pleasant way but it was the most powerful.* A string of blood splashed onto Flint's chest whilst reloading and he felt it soak in against his stomach. The .50 cal gunner next to him had fallen victim to a sharp burst of fire to his exposed shoulders. The loader stared at his best friend who lay still on the rubble.

"Keep firing!" a soldier commanded. Flint aimed his rifle steadily at the bottom of the refinery.

KWA!

The oil pole shattered into a million pieces and rained down, black liquid and blazing flames crashing into the Germans below. The oil explosion not only set off a vigorous blast but the fire engulfed everything in a five metre radius.

Including the Germans.

Flint hated it. He hated seeing people just like him, an enemy or not, having to be gunned down to the floor rather than die a different way. Too much had happened since the shipwreck in the English Channel and if he had known what was coming when he enlisted, he would never have dreamed or even dared to.

"Move up!"

A sixteen man army climbed over the debris and charged, oblivious to the fact that there were still more Germans out there. They hurryingly jogged to the building in front, another similar office block. Deep thuds echoed inside…the enemy footsteps were hoofing up and down. Only some scatters of gunfire zipped between them however they all made it alive, laying their backs against the exterior walls.

"Last block!" Flint heard Brighton shout. "Rodriguez, take your squad inside and clear it out! Go!"

Lieutenant Rodriguez nodded and checked his shotgun, examining briefly the barrel, which melted frost on the windows. He kicked down the door and burst in, followed closely by a line of soldiers almost like a long, winding snake. The atmosphere began to fall silent. One shot was heard. Then two. Flint and Hayden remained leaning against the wall as the all clear from the inside sounded. They peered into the doorway, seeing one German sprawled across the floor without an arm and another at the back door slumped over the doormat.

"Bet he's as not as cold as we are now," muttered Flint. The others around him let out a well waited for laugh. Rodriguez came out back into the light, his eyes heavy with dread and exhaustion.

"All clear."

Sergeant Brighton's radio crackled in,

"Bravo Six, this is HQ, the Americans are sending Yankee Six Four in on your position. Do not fire. I repeat, do not fire. Over."

"Copy."

A pair of Sherman tanks bustled in from the treeline. Tearing at tree branches, which cracked onto the ground. Snow chugged out from the engines, a deep noise grunted as it slowly lumbered forwards. A cheer was heard from Rodriguez's squad as the tanks rolled down the road.

"Bravo Six, this is Yankee Six Four," a deep Californian accent echoed. *"Clear the rest of the refinery up ahead of us, don't want no mines under these tracks. Over."*

"Roger, Yankee Six Four. We're moving up now. Over," recalled Brighton with his own British accent. "Bravo Six, on me!"

Flint held his rifle in one hand and followed, scattering down the road with Hayden and the rest. He leaped over a pile of ash and molten bodies, the smell putting him off and contaminating the area. The squad suddenly came to a halt by a crossroad just behind the refinery. One road led down into the overhanging, frozen forest, the other winding between a mixture of high strands of icy grass and trees. They all were desperate to escape the stench of death. Flint looked on the opposite side of the road. Rodriguez and his team were climbing a frozen stairwell up an uncleared office building.

"What are they doing?" Hayden moaned, the cold air puffing from his mouth.

"Probably scouting it out, don't know why though," answered Cole quietly. Not much had been heard of him recently. His injuries had crippled him to a point where he found it hard to run, even worse walk! Bravo Six knelt down next to the pavement and watched as shimmers and reflections crossed the building. A window suddenly smashed open.

Rodriguez had used the butt of his gun to batter it free. He peered out; nodded, then alerted all was clear with his arm sticking out the busted window.

BOOM!

A sudden bolt smashed into the offices and let out a ferocious explosion. Rodriguez's arm blasted off and flew into the fence behind Hayden's head. The room the men were in exploded into a thousand pieces of rubble.

"Lie down and get cover!" Cole managed to blurt out.

Bricks rained down around them. The crumbling dissipated. Howls of pain were heard, but after a short while, disappeared. A deep grumbling sound suddenly attracted their attention…once again; an unwelcoming hood of a Tiger Tank greeted them. The front was the vilest thing any allied soldier ever dreamed of coming across. The twisted black metal sprawled along the front with tiny holes poking through; the MG gunners' main killing machine.

"All you guys okay?" exclaimed Flint, as he lay dead still next to the road.

The cannon of the tank pivoted directly towards Brighton. He slowly rose up, not realising death was metres away.

"Sir, *MOVE!*"

Brighton whipped his head around to see the tank only metres from him. A twisted, looming shadow over him. Lieutenant Cole burst in from behind…barging him out the way as an almighty shell whizzed past their ears. Flint leapt up, distracting the tank from one side from the right by firing stray shots. To the left, Cole put Brighton on his shoulders and *ran*. Scott snatched the radio from the ground and wailed into it: "Yankee Six Four! This is Bravo Six! A Tiger Tank has just engaged with us down the road! Can you support, over?"

"No problem, Bravo Six. Comin' in hot," a muffled voice answered.

"I got you!" Cole muttered as he burst towards the nearest fence. His strides were long, sprinting across the cracked concrete in the most desperate manner.

BANG! BANG! BANG! BANG!

Four red holes ripped open in Cole's back.

"Arghhhhh…" he moaned as Brighton collapsed off his shoulders. Both men's helmets toppled to the floor. Cole fell to the ground, his clothes beginning to soak in blood as he tried one more time to rise up…

To finish the mission.

BANG! BANG! BANG!

The Tiger Tanks machine gun pounded into the lone lieutenant. Flint's face froze. Cole dropped to the floor.

BOOM!

A sudden bright red flash dawned around them; followed by the sky raining burnt metal. Flint looked up. The Tiger Tank had completely split in half, the lid lying across the road. His ears were pierced with a screeching sound. It stung.

Yankee Six Four rumbled past him dripping small trickles of diesel. Cheering could be heard inside. Howls of laughter and American songs echoed as they ascended up to the crossroad, accelerating around the curve and stopping in a thick texture of mud. Flint picked up his pistol from the floor. He wearily staggered up and headed over to Cole who was gasping for air. A large sheet of lead lay across him.

"Sir! Sir!" Flint said, his heart throbbing in sorrow. He impatiently lifted the sheet and threw it to the side as it splashed in thin oil.

"Flint…"

Hayden ran out of cover from behind the fence and headed to the downed lieutenant.

"He's gone," Flint blankly muttered as he walked over to the burning axis tank.

Hayden froze.

"What?"

"I said he's gone! What more do you want!" He pushed Hayden with force whilst walking past.

A sudden German soldier trudged unarmed from under the tank, a smear of blood and ash across his face. He spoke in broken English.

"I surren—" Flint shot him through the chest and walked over to Aaron who looked unusually downcast.

"Man." Aaron spat onto the road. "Those Nazis took Cole early, that's for sure."

"He's gone now. We have to move on," Flint replied, staring at Hayden who tried to revive him.

"Just shows you, Rodriguez and his boys are idiots. Exposing us like that."

"Well," Aaron began and sighed, "it's not like there's much of them left anyway."

Both looked at the lone hand at the fence.

"They're all too dead to realise anyway."

"Mitchell, Addington!" called a voice. The pair turned around, seeing Brighton steadily making his way over in injured fashion.

"You good, sir? Looks like you got pretty shaken up back there." Aaron chuckled.

"Just picked up a knock. That's all."

Flint watched Brighton secretly try to cover up the blood dripping out from his stomach. He called out to ditch the attention, "Scott! We need the radio!"

He came running from behind the fence, his helmet bouncing up and down on his head. He handed over the burnt radio to the sergeant.

"Don't know if it still works, Sarge. It's been mashed up pretty bad…" Scott implied. Brighton nodded slowly. The squad stood silently in a circle next to the rubble of the destroyed building; the fire from the tank warming in the chills of the coming evening. They were beginning to become too mentally shattered to communicate…and now with Cole gone…Brighton was off his leash. Aside from that, hope was quickly restored as Brighton fixed the radio. Like always, it crackled into its familiar deep frequency.

"HQ, this is Bravo Six, uh…we just encountered a hidden Tiger Tank. Sergeant Rodriguez's squad and Lieutenant Cole have both been confirmed dead. We presume Private Heaton is with Sergeant Raymond on the north side of the refinery. Us and Yankee Six Four are waiting for orders, over."

"We copy that, Bravo Six…" The soldiers waited eagerly. *"Your last assignment has been confirmed…"*

14 – The Unlucky

S o then I said to this guy "I might as well be the barman myself! I mean, what else was there!" Hayden laughed whilst leaning on the table.

It was a month later.

Bravo Six had crossed into Germany a few weeks back under the protection of the main allied advance. They hadn't engaged in combat once since the refineries; however, the sacrificial death of Cole had troubled them all deeply…now they are stationed at Dedenbach, Germany, preparing for their final assault of the war. Twenty kilometres away is Remagen. In Remagen? Well, let Sergeant Brighton explain that…

Flint Mitchell looked back up, standing around a large oak table; it was covered with a huge map and tactical war documents. They were inside an average military tent. Coloured in dark green and beige, a very simple layout had greeted them. He wore a vest and jeans both of which looked much smarter than their regular uniforms. Bruises marked his body. Long deep cuts slowly formed into scars. He just wanted to go home.

Private Heaton had re-joined the squad, his green beanie still placed on his head with his typical northern accent. The sound of weary soldiers and allied vehicles could be heard rumbling outside winding between narrow village roads and dried-out water fountains. Aaron, Scott and Hayden all surrounded the map too, chatting hysterically.

"Quite an interesting story you've got there, Hayden," a voice mumbled.

Sergeant Brighton emerged from the thin flaps of the tent, his presence silencing the squad members as he allowed the light, which followed to illuminate the inside. His rifle was slung around his burnt shoulder. Boots polished, buttons up and medals attached. He looked as serious as ever…a small bit of him was still trying to comprehend that this would be his final ever assignment.

"Mission brief," he sturdily welcomed.

The squad gathered around.

"Let's see what we got…" muttered Flint, his hands struggling not to shake. He thought to himself about this, *if only there was a way to control it…*

"As most of you probably know, only a handful of bridges still stand across the Rhine River. Why's the Rhine so important to us you may ask? Well, without it there's no way of reaching the heart of Germany…that is Berlin. These bridges are most likely smothered in dynamite charges and they must *not* fall. An allied attack is commencing tomorrow on one of the mains. Ludendorff Bridge."

Flint studied the map ahead. Ludendorff was a huge structure scaping across two mainland territories and had a German air hangar not too far from it.

Great.

Another danger to look out for.

Planes.

"Our job is to locate and disarm the charges. From here to Remagen, Yankee Six Four will transport us along with Delta Company twenty kilometres northeast. We arrive in the small fishing port village at the base of Ludendorff. From there? Local informants will reveal the locations of the dynamite. Orders from HQ will follow." Brighton pointed down at various points on the map. The soldiers nodded anxiously and headed out before being interrupted once more.

"There's gonna be no snow by the way, lads."

A sudden cheer was kick started by Aaron. Flint followed in with the rest. It felt good to smile. Even be out the cold. He then brushed his hair back, his hands still too numb from weeks ago to even feel it. *Only a couple of days left*, he reassured himself with. Grabbing his rifle, which leaned against the side of the tent, he pulled away the entrance flaps. Rays of light beamed in his eyes as he stepped out. Their tent was pitched on the outskirts of an insignificant farming village. Dedenbach had wide, open plains, which would be golden when harvested. German families had picnics on a regular basis, eager to see the magnificent sunset at dusk. Now it was a wrecked wasteland; dumped with rotting trees and twisted steel.

Shells had left gaping holes scattered around the village. Long outstretched ditches were filled with dead Jews and German deserters who were still fresh due to the axis retreating so quick. The farms were now swamplands, which had become a living playground for parasites and fleas. Apart from the nearby fields, most was intact. The main body of the village lay slumped on the side of a small valley. Its classic brick houses were deserted and small passage-like pathways were like the motorways of the village.

Flint Mitchell strolled into a familiar looking building, its walls painted in pale stripes and a huge signboard outside. He remembered now. *La Chocolatiere Du Panier*...the chocolate shop he had blown to bits whilst in the Sherman at Bayeux. It looked very similar. To him it seemed like years from then.

"Flint!" Hayden called from one of the tables.

"Good to see you," he spoke back.

Flint yanked a chair back and finally rested his scarred legs. He opened his mouth:

"No. This place does not sell chocolate anymore," Hayden quickly interrupted.

Flint blankly replied, "I wasn't going to ask that."

"Oh, carry on then, I guess." Hayden said.

"Does this place still serve...?"

"You're joking."

Flint leaned back on his chair and laughed.

"You know what..." Hayden couldn't find the words and sighed. "Okay...it hasn't sold anything since 1940, apparently 'cause of the lack of food, but we got one of our boys behind the counter selling canteens of water and beer." He nodded at a burly bloke inspecting his pistol on the table next to them. "Always wanted to be a 'shop owner'."

"Oh, yeah? Him? Looks more like a boxer to me. I mean, look at him."

Both turned their heads to see him sipping a white coffee, quite ferociously actually.

"Can't really disagree there..." Hayden muttered. "Anyway, there's a guy I want you to meet. Otto. Proper brick wall, mate. He might look like nothing much, but you'll see what I mean."

Flint watched as his friend stood up, adjusting the strap on his helmet before walking into a hidden back room back behind the empty counter. A minute later, Otto appeared in the hallway tiptoeing down to their table. He was unique on first sight. A white spotted bow tie was fitted exactly straight across his neck and he had a faint moustache like a stereotypical Frenchman. Shining boots was followed by an impeccable clean tuxedo. They shook hands and introduced each other. Otto's hands were cold, frightened almost as he slowly slipped them into his blazer pocket. All three men sat down. Flint had the sensation of the stranger scanning him intensely…

"You're the only civilian I've seen here," Flint spoke quietly. "Where's everyone else? Do you have a family?"

Otto's face morphed into a deep phase of sudden, unexpected depression. He glanced down at the dusty table.

"I…" He froze for a moment before breathing in a gulp of air. "I am the only one left."

Hayden and Flint were taken aback a little to find the correct words. His green eyes were clouding up with the pain and violence.

"What happened? Was it our guys that did it?" Flint asked intently.

"Last week my family and I were lying on the fields…watching the tiny puffy clouds above on that brilliant sunny day. The sky was tranquil, the rolling grass the greenest it had ever become. The crops a golden haze. It was perfect."

Otto smiled to himself whilst staring outside at the misery of what joy had become.

A lone tear trickled down his cheek.

"Just me, my wife Julie, and the two kids Axel and Greta, enjoying ourselves in the realms of spring. Lunchtime greeted us and we made our way back to the village, already planning the wonderful meal ahead of us. We arrived and the most dreadful sight welcomed our eyes. The Nazis had come. Half a dozen jeeps rounded up all the men, woman and children up in the centre square, their eyes clogged with horrific fear. We instantly dropped behind a fallen tree trunk where the infants would always play; scared to death in case we were seen. I told my family to run to the nearby woods on my call. It would save their lives. Anyway, to the woods entrance from the trunk was tall, long strands of grass which would cover their every move even if there was the odd stumble. The woods were not far at all, only around twenty metres. The time was right. They ran through the grass, I watched them disperse out of my grip; knowing whatever would happen now would never be in my power. I saw Axel's hand wave to alert me that…they had made it safe and unseen. I signalled them to hide wherever possible: trees, holes, grass, bushes, caves. With them gone, I refocused and crawled to the first house of the village. Mr and Mrs Heimlich's house was empty; I scavenged for anything, from a simple screwdriver to an axe, at least. But nothing.

"I silently winded out from the back door and followed the hedges to Mr Fischer's household, the popular local lumberjack. Sure enough to my surprise,

I ripped open the wardrobes and discovered a Karabiner 98K under a stack of jeans. I had been there once last July, looking for a good price for some of his seemingly endless amount of chopped oak. We were all a tight knit community and all friends; I had to save them. In less than a second, I found myself darting upstairs and staring out from Mr Fischer's bedroom window, a perfect view of the central square as I blended in with the curtains. I slowly tilted the window the slightest bit forward…before slotting the heavy rifle through. I waited for the right time to strike."

Flint listened in more tensely by the second. It reminded him of his first encounters with the Nazis at his uncle's house, at the very start of his campaign.

"My fellow brothers and sisters were forced into a large clumped circle, the soldiers completely surrounding them from all sides. 'Why were Germans doing this to us? We are Germans as well' my initial thoughts were. That was until I saw Mr Johnsen step out from the shadows…and join the Nazis. He had betrayed us. Ever since his dastardly works on burning our wheat fields had been exposed, he had hated us as a community ever since. He was due to leave the village by popular demand last week, but he had persuaded us to leave it 'til another seven days. See what he meant now. He sought out every person there, informing the main commander about their vicious acts against country and monarch. Of course, this was not true; in fact, he was lying by the highest degree. To top it off, he concluded they were all Jews too, a crime most likely worthy of instant execution. They had done nothing against the country and faced the consequences. They certainly weren't Jews, either. I scoped in on the commander's head, seeing that dirty, disgusting, yet ruthless swastika sit on his folded cap. Screaming was suddenly heard from out of nowhere.

"Who was it? My…my family suddenly appeared. They were dragged across the square and chucked into the middle with the rest, like worthless animals. My whole body overpowered with rage. My whole body fuelled with the roaring feeling of hatred. I pulled the trigger. I rocked as the recoil nearly tore my shoulder. But nothing happened at all. A blank had been fired. I ducked behind the window ledge in the upmost shock. To my luck, the Nazis had luckily not heard it. How had it happened though? I had just checked the magazine and saw everything was correct! A grunt was heard behind me. I whipped back and froze still. Mr Fischer charged at me with full force.

"I smacked him with the butt of the gun but we still smashed through the window together. Both of us flipped backwards into a lethal free-fall. We cascaded onto the pavement below with shards of razor glass raining around us. Turns out, Mr Fischer was also part of this betrayal scheme too.

"I blacked out for a second, before seeing Fischer loom over me and grinning. My vision drained, hearing whined and total sense sucked out of me. My head forced itself to the left. Screaming echoed in my ears as gunshots pierced and rang in my head. I witnessed the townsfolk instantly massacred. My wife and children riddled. Enough. The rage built up and exploded in me once more. I snatched a nearby shard of glass and fended myself. I never actually attacked him; however, I waved the makeshift weapon near his face. Then I ran."

Otto started to cry quietly, his tears falling onto the table. He was heartbroken from everything.

"The…the…" He breathed in deeply, almost like a sigh, before wiping away the tears from his face. "The Nazis watched everything and it wasn't long before they started shooting at me, also. I managed to escape and run back to the fallen tree where we started. They came out of the valley in their jeeps, an endless amount; seemed like hundreds of them, scouting the smallest bit of grain. Little did they know I hid inside the dark tree trunk even when they searched it underneath.

"When I returned back, the place was silent and looted. Nothing moved and it was the strangest yet saddest thing that had ever met my eyes. To think that only yesterday it was bustling with joyful life to now dead, empty bodies. I thought it couldn't get any worse even when I found everyone lying still in the central square. Massacred for nothing. I buried everyone of one of them, every single friend. My wife. My son and daughter."

He revealed his dirt-stained hands from under the table before nodding at the muddy shovel, which lay perched against the wall.

"When I got back to the village after a whole day of digging, you and your artillery blew the fields around here to bits. All day it was constant drumming and the rain began to fall as well. Luckily, I knew a safe spot right here beneath our feet. Let me show you."

Otto lifted the table up and dragged it to one side, the loud banging noise disturbing the soldier who silently sat sipping his coffee. He tore at the broken floorboard and a small trapdoor gracefully revealed itself.

"I've been in here for the last week."

Flint looked into the dark, candle-lit basement illuminated by a dire flame.

Scrunches of wrappers littered the cold, concrete floor and a small fire pit sat in one corner; burning away next to stacks of paper.

"I really don't know what to say..." Flint implied whilst looking at the ground. He added slowly, "All I know is that I do kind of know how part of it feels. To be left alone and to see your family killed."

The distraught German contemplated this, his hands shaking whilst lost in deep thought. He looked helpless, melancholic mostly.

"I do not like this." He wiped several tears from his eyes and took a deep breath. "We better get going before more Nazis come and bomb this place to its eternal end."

Flint looked through the cracked window and gazed at the sky, which slowly ascended into dusk. It was like two different worlds, the sky and ground. Down here, it was blood and mud...but up there? The moon glimmering was its only noticeable appearance.

Otto straightened his jacket before walking slowly over to his trapdoor.

"Match?"

Hayden dug into his pockets and tossed over a stick. He froze for a moment before asking, "You sure you want to stay in one of the houses? Looks a lot more comfor—"

"No, no, no." He made a cross with his hands. He added, "Too dangerous. Like I said, they're everywhere...have a good night, Mr Flint and Mr Hayden."

Both soldiers nodded and watched as Otto climbed in with a newly struck torch. Sparks lingered out as he swiftly drew the trapdoor to a close. Hayden smirked and turned to Flint with a gleeful manner. He took off his helmet before announcing, "Orders from Sergeant, Flint. Report back to him. He wants a quick check-up for the next operation at the Rhine. Besides from that, I've got good and bad news."

"What now?" he replied.

"The good news is the Russians just launched one of their riskiest battles of the war. It's starting off with some infantry charges first, however."

"And the bad news?"

"We're on night patrol..."

15 – Red Entrance

Pvt. Dimitri Revinslav
Soviet Union
2ⁿᵈ Belorussian Front
10ᵗʰ Army

3,297 KM EAST
SOUTHERN LITHUANIA
11:30 AM

Hey, Private Revinslav! Look! Our brothers are in the skies!

A deep howl of anticipated and victorious laughter followed from Field Marshall Morozov. I gazed up at the magnificent red planes soaring up high, prowling the air like Moscow eagles. The few sunlight rays that shone silked through the thick black clouds of the day and shimmered in my eyes. Their engines whirred and swooped towards the near city of Alytus in total skill and precision.

"What make are they?" I asked enthusiastically. Ivan strolled in from behind and patted me on the back.

"Bell P-39 Airacobra. Best of the best, I tell you."

My friend Ivan was scruffily dressed. A muddy red uniform was the first sight upon eyed however; it was the burnt back and ripped sleeves that revealed he had been in heavy combat recently. He had dull, green eyes with a scarred skinhead; just like me. All of us wore grey wolf Ushankas, our beloved Soviet symbol knitted in on the furry front and long earflaps that helped us in the bitter, freezing winters. We had worn the same one since 1942!

The Field Marshall staggered over to me and Ivan, wheezing as he did so. He fumbled around in his trouser pockets before pulling out a grimy, half-full vodka bottle and slowly poured the contents in his mouth; in one go. He wiped his short white beard and pointed towards me and Ivan.

"You two!"

"Yes, sir?" I replied boldly. Ivan clenched the killer PPSHs in his hands. We had commonly seen officers executing their own in public for simple mistakes.

"Where's your sergeant?"

"Smirnov, sir? Killed back in Minsk after a shell hit him. It's not as if he had any chance anyway, we had no guns to attack the city with, so we charged in empty handed."

"One of the few disappointments this nation faces..." His face fell, then suddenly uplifted on a passionate roar, "And it's because of those Nazis!"

Morozov sneered in disgust. He kicked a brick into the wall near me, then added, "Well, let's see if the grace of our beloved communist nation blesses you with the hope of survival dis time..."

BOOM!

Suddenly, the very earth around us shattered like an earthquake! I went ducking for cover behind a pile of burnt rubble; trying to not expose myself from out the cover of the wall. Others just like me fell to their feet and dived behind the barbed wire.

"What was that?" one private whimpered.

He was a coward from the start...everyone could see it. It was his first day on the force. He was barely a man yet, roughly sixteen, and still had a photograph of his family in his chest pocket where everyone could see. Ha!

He wouldn't survive a night.

My thoughts were dragged back to the conflict as Colonel Aleksandr replied in a great, commanding voice. "It's the artillery of our comrades back at the lake. They are bombing the city. Destroying the Germans as we speak!"

I peeped my head over the broken wall which gave us cover. There were around one hundred of us behind that twenty-metre concrete structure. Directly in front, however, lay the entrance gate to Alytus, looking too similar to a medieval opening. To capture Alytus was our next objective in 'Operation Bagration'. This was part of the counter-attack from Moscow when the Nazis made the fatal mistake of invading our homeland. The hardest Soviet tank battle ever conducted after Kursk; had only been fought here three years ago...resulting in a clever Nazi victory. We had managed to push them back to Lithuania though, which was incredible despite our millions of deaths in the process. Twenty-five million civilians and eleven million soldiers. All dead. We haven't even reached Poland yet!

Unlit torches hung from the gate barriers and besides them stood multiple, half-bombed four storey buildings, which inherited smears and stains of molten shades of jet black. A huge blaze must've ripped through and smashed the windows into gaping holes. Of course, we all knew who created it and now took position with MG42s at the windows. Dirty Nazis; they were using this as the first defensive point from the city of Alytus. To add to our flustered rage, dead guards and civilian bodies (littered with bullet holes) lay lifeless at the entrance. The Nazis had massacred them upon arrival and not have even been bothered to dump them into graves. If that was bad, the Vidzgiris Forest loomed over behind us. The howls and wails of dead, forgotten humans could be noticed distinctively throughout the land. 60,000 innocents had been taken from nearby Lithuanian villages and dumped into Vidzgiris. The Germans had murdered every last one.

Alytus produced dark illuminated flames, which scorched over the horizon; funnels of cloggy black smoke pummelled into the clouds. It was a common urban city for the most part with stacks upon stacks of houses crammed into dense streets. It might've been a joy a week earlier, however now it was a living nightmare: with a stenching concentration camp just to its left by the grimy canals. We had heard of hoards of families battered into gas chambers to meet a gruesome end. These Germans brutally destroy anything in their way. They were savages in fine cloak.

Morozov mentally squared up and measured the distance between us and the armed buildings.

One hundred metres.

Like a strike of pure relief, in the distance marched two hundred of our courageous comrades singing in all their glory the songs of Stalin. They arrived finally in perfectly ordered lines and quickly descended into ducked positions. Messages of hope and greetings among us spread like wildfire as we thanked our brothers-in-arms for coming. Unfortunately, they looked sleep-deprived and mentally exhausted, furthermore, many were limping with bloodied legs and bandages despite their immense singing. I approached one who had a spotted scarf dangled around his neck and a missing Ushanka.

"Here, drink, brother," I reassured him as my hand gave him a canteen of vodka.

"Thank you. My name's Fedorov Konstantiv."

He winced in pain whilst we shook hands firmly.

"Dimitri Revinslav."

"Well, it's a pleasu—"

Fedorov covered his mouth and spluttered into his elbow. Snatching my bottle back off me, he moaned in grief and hurt. I was a little taken back, frankly, but he tapped me on the shoulder and delivered one last sentence.

"We've just come from Leningrad and let me tell you first hand; it's a mess, Dimitri. Six hundred thousand dead and a skyline full of collapsed towers!"

"How long you've been fighting?"

"Three years now, since yesterday. I've been through five different platoons. Every one ends in the same story! A barrage of shells or unexpected ambushes top the results. Not one of them made it out."

"Prepare ze weapons!" one ill-faced colonel shrieked in the midst of our conversations. A dense fog emerged over us and lingered as we hammered our guns ready for battle. Clanking of metal and thuds of feet could be heard as we awaited the onslaught that came quietly like poison in the wind. We all eyed the same target: Alytus' gates which led to the central city.

Heavy breathing penetrated the silence despite the thudding of some beating their chests. The assault was about to commence.

Like a hungry bear, Field Marshall Morozov blistered into deep wine red and burst into severe rage…

"Brothers! There is only one thing slowing us down from reaching Berlin after this attack…" He pointed majestically at the Germans in the string of buildings.

"It will be mountains of their own dead piled on top of each other as they retreat!

"Get ready, men!

"We will destroy their fascist Reich!

"However many struggles we may encounter, let this be the most glorious day you will ever live!

"Our almighty leaders have sent you here for ripping apart Hitler's legions!

"Forward, comrades!

"Do not count days, do not count miles, count only the number of Germans you have killed!

"Do not show mercy to the merciless and kill all the vermin!

"Kill! Kill!

"Execute every crawling one of them and not one must escape!

"Fight for your nation, for your home!

"Engulf the Germans with the brutal wrath in which no army can ever match!

"Defend Russia!

"Not one step back!

"Forward, comrades! Forward!

"For mother Russia!"

Every one of us erupted into a graceful uproar, one that fuelled us for the coming slaughter. The signature battle cry emerged in the wind, slowly getting louder and louder over every word.

"*Urra…urra…urra…urra…urra…*"

Silence rippled in the air.

"*Urra!!!*"

All three hundred of us screamed in rage and fury as we leapt out of cover, fuelled by Morozov's glorious speech. We strode across the plain with jingling satchels of ammo and the hoofing of boots.

"Ha! They are too scared to even dare open fire on us!" he exclaimed.

Me and Ivan burst across the misty field together surrounded by our comrades and brothers-in-arms. Alarm bells suddenly began to ring in the city; chimes of surprise and shock came from the defending Germans as they witnessed the Red Army barrelling towards them.

BANG! BANG! BANG!

A scatter of gunfire slammed the soldier next to me into the ground dead. It didn't stop there. Strings of hammering bullets leapt past me and lit up my men. Guns were thrown in the air and blood splashed in my face as I tripped over a body and plummeted to the floor. I couldn't hear anything. I could just feel the dirt fling into my eyes and the warmth of the bullets drag across my body.

Ha. Who was I? I couldn't just let a trip and skim destine my fate.

Hordes of soldiers shoved past me and dispersed into the fog. Lines of yellow zipped past and thudded into my comrades next to me whilst I stumbled back up. Using my PPSH, I randomly drive solid shots towards the buildings in hope of one of them falling to the floor – so I could finish them off myself. Ivan bolted towards me with a painful expression.

"Keep going! For victory!" He helped me up properly and we burst across the wet grass together.

My heart nearly exploded in beating acceleration whilst passing more soldiers crawling for survival. Screams of anguish and screams of passion were muffled by the damage to my ears. I witnessed Field Marshall dash past mumbling hateful phrases. But he wasn't running towards the gate.

I vaguely saw him through the fog as he yanked that whimpering private from behind a rock. It was bizarre at the fullest. Despite the raging battle, Morozov slashed him across the face and shot him through the photograph in his chest. Surprised, the boy held his chest and crumpled to one side.

"Dimitri! Concentrate!" Ivan shrieked among the other howls for a medic. "*Bazuka!!!*"

Grenadier Mikhailov placed an RPG on his shoulder and carefully aimed the barrel towards the second German building.

"Revinslav, move!"

SWOOSH!

The shell swept past my face and smashed into the dull grey building with a mighty crack, which echoed over the screams. The building crumbled from its roots; toppling over into the field in front. Scarlet flames engulfed the ruined bricks as me and my men staggered once more forward over piles of our own.

I hip-fired my PPSH until it had run clean and watched my bullets zip into the windows. The gun burnt in my hands however, I kept running between the smoke and chaos.

"Medic!" a lame soldier cried as he tried to patch his multiple gunshot wounds. A shot blasted through his chin and out his shoulder.

I hurled myself behind a twisted pile of metal, feeling sick to the core, and watched countless bodies stack on top of each other. I had to do something before my whole legion was wiped out! I felt the bump of someone behind me.

"They're pointing right at us! Run! The wall's just there!"

"Go!" I yelled back at Ivan.

Through the mist of the fog, a slender barrel caught my sight and let loose, spraying hundreds of bullets in my direction. The soldier next to me screamed wildly as a couple of bullets tore his entire arm off.

RATATATATA!

I kept running tirelessly and collapsed ten metres from the wall in shock and agony at the sight that bestowed me. My breathing was the loudest thing I could hear as Ivan fumbled with his chest on the ground. Pools of blood surrounded him. The MG42s bullets scattered around however didn't once struck us! Mercy had come from the reassurance of Stalin!

"Ivan!"

My heart raced as I covered up the wounds on his legs and chest. Several bullets had ripped straight through and left gaping, empty holes. I searched his pockets for a cloth of any sort. Any! A string granted my hand in his back trouser pocket.

"You're—"

His eyes were closed and still. Morozov shrieked under the drumming of gunfire,

"Run!"

An explosion swiped me of my knees and battered me to the ground. I inhaled cordite and gunpowder as a looming object blocked out the sun. The light dimmed. Glancing to all sides, my eyes witnessed our soldiers dashing back to halfway and collapsing to the floor. Some were still crashing back down by the whistling bullets.

A crack nearly split my ears and the terrain around shifted into a deep, dark silhouette. Dead bodies surrounded me on the grass. I realised I was the only living one there.

Suddenly, the most intense feeling shattered my skull and split through my lung and legs. Those Germans were still shooting and their bullets had ripped into me. I desperately wheezed and began to crawl out of the firing range. The shooting stopped as swiftly as it had started.

That was because one of the buildings had begun to cascade...over to my side.

With inner acceleration, I heaved myself over to the light, knowing that the building wouldn't land there. However, with the adrenaline and rush of battle wiped from me for the second, an unnatural, burning pain stretched across my left ear and stung like a hammered nail.

I felt the side of my head, however there was nothing there. Those Germans had shot my ear off entirely.

"Dimitri Revinslav!" screeched Morozov slowly.

The first bricks thudded onto my head…followed by a huge array of burning and sparking metal. In my final moments, with the world crashing all around me, I let my hand grip like an iron to my beloved PPSH and Ushanka.

For Russia.

16 – From All Corners

Pvt. Flint Mitchell
British 3rd Infantry Division
Delta Company
Bravo Six

T his is Yankee Six Four at your service; we're on the road leaving Dedenbach. Let us know when you're ready, over.

"Copy that, we're on our way."

Six gloomy faced, war-torn men scoured their rooms and collected the essentials in a mix of exhaustion and early morning sickness. Rifle, overalls, spare ammunition, couple of canteens of water, tinned cans, pistol, helmet, knife, grenades and a simple first aid pouch were all quickly stuffed into combat packs. One weary soldier who wore a camo beanie raised his voice above the noises of scrunching and thudding.

"We headin' out now, sir?"

The sergeant nodded. "Yes. Follow me."

Flint Mitchell and Hayden Hendrix heaved the ever-expanding bags across their shoulders. The straps rubbed in and caused irritation however the job had to be done. Flint held his M1 Garand in his hands after checking the barrel and joined Brighton as they jogged out the building.

The sergeant strained to open the metal entrance door and a gush of blistering yet cold wind whooshed into their faces. Dedenbach was quiet. The only peep of noise was the channel of footsteps that separated them from eerie silence. Approximately, it was only four o'clock in the morning, but dawn was on the horizon and chilling clouds stripped across the lightening skies above. Bravo Six were the only ones awake and moving. The main task force still lay waiting for orders in the forgotten village; gradually becoming increasingly weary of enemy airstrikes or imminent invasion. Flint rubbed his hands for warmth and clenched the rifle in his hands as they set off down the road; the lane obliterated with bullet holes and cracked buildings. Blood was still smeared across the walls and cobblestone.

Distant cries could be heard in the direction in which they strode. Goosebumps riddled across Flint's body as they became ever so louder. An assault? They'd have to be the first ones to engage head on.

The snake of soldiers winded through the main road until the first glimpse of a Sherman tank had been caught.

"That's them," Brighton muttered.

Four rugged Americans stretched out across the length of their grimy tank; resting comfortably on the machine guns that gazed on its surroundings up top. They all smoked cigarettes whilst peering down on a lone figure chained to a nearby pine tree. He looked distraught and had a slender build. A blue cap sat on his head, which covered his infected cuts and bruises. He looked about twenty but his deep experience looked as if he had soared past that years ago. Groans of entertainment rippled across the tank crew. As Flint's squad marched in nearer, the growing conversation became more audibly clear to the ear.

The tank gunner shook his head and took the cigarette out of his mouth. He waved his hands as he spoke, a trail of polluting air followed. "Listen carefully now. I'm gonna put a bullet in your head if you don't start tellin' us where the rest of you are. Just tell us…where are the *other* Germans?"

"*Jestem polskim partyzantem! Nie jestem Niemcen! Pozwol mi odejsc!*" the man shrieked back.

The soldiers were stunned. They looked at one another in the most utterly confused manner. The driver jumped off from the hood of the tank with a thump onto the grass. He rubbed the grease of his burnt sleeves.

"What'd he say, Sarge?"

"Does it look like I speak Third Reich?" the commander replied with a raised eyebrow.

Aaron White burst past Flint and scurried towards the Americans, swinging his rifle. An expression of hope rippled across his desperate face. He came to a stumbling halt face-to-face with the commander.

"Private White," he greeted, seeing the war scars dragged across the American's eye and cheek.

"Bravo Six?"

"That's us, sir."

"Name's Beckett."

Aaron nodded as he paced over to the chained, slumped figure. Flint introduced himself with the crew and wandered to Aaron as he spoke.

"He's Polish, Commander Beckett."

The chains were bolted off and the Polish man collapsed to his knees taking in deep gulps of air. He wiped the sweat of his forehead with battered hands.

"You could've told me!" Beckett sighed at the driver.

"*Nazywam sie Nowak Zielinsk*—" he spluttered to the side with an hoarse, chesty cough. "*Jestem czescia grupy opuru Lesni w Polsce.*"

Aaron nodded his head in clear understanding and helped the man up to his feet.

"Aaron?" called Scott.

"He says his name is Nowak Zielinsk. Part of some resistance movement in Poland—"

Nowak interrupted in a deep, shaken voice with wide eyes and muttered in Polish once more. Aaron took a step back at the words that he spoke. *It couldn't be!* he thought.

"The Germans. They know we're advancing on Remagen this evening!" the Brit cried out. A wave of uncertainty and dread spread across the two groups like wild fire. Flint watched on, disturbed. "He says to call off any planned attacks immediately! They've set up heavy defences throughout the bridge and ditched the dynamite!"

It was now Flint who spoke up amongst the other mumbles of fear. He first had to make sure who exactly this man claimed to be.

"Ask him how he got here."

Aaron took off his helmet and confirmed with Nowak. The Polish man rubbed his sodden face and revealed a Frommer Stop Auto from his back pocket. It was a simple weapon. Originally a Hungarian handgun, Nowak had converted it to a fully auto machine pistol. Jet black and rapidly fast, it had an extended magazine sticking out from the oak handle and stored fifteen rounds of ammunition.

"He says that since the Germans had cut off their communication lines in Poland, he volunteered to travel across Europe to tell of upcoming axis plans. This was his last assignment: tellin' us. He's on his way back to fight in the forests."

"Woah, woah, woah. Hang on a minute, let's not get ahead of ourselves 'cause of some stranger," announced Hayden curiously.

"Yeah," spoke another American on the tank. "How'd we know he's not lying?"

Aaron translated this.

"*Chca wiedziec, czy klamiesz, czy nie.*"

The Polish soldier stared at them. His arms slung over to his back and he slowly removed his coal black coat and shirt. White skin met red. An engraved Star of David had been burnt into his back, moulds of black and inferno red, which left deep, dark scars.

That said enough.

Brighton pondered and spoke, "The Germans must've got to him."

The squad looked at the ground; desperate to reach an idea of the next plan. Flint chucked his water bottle to Nowak. He nodded his head in gratitude.

"I'll get word back to HQ at Paris and see what they suggest. For now though, take five. I'll be back in a bit."

"Yes, sir," the men responded as they leaned against the waiting tank. Sergeant Brighton slung his rifle across his shoulders and slowly made his way back into central Dedenbach.

Something suddenly waded in the distance like a mirage just as he disappeared behind the first house. A brush against the ferns; collided with a silent whisper in the looming trees.

There was no time to further investigate.

"Enemy troops!" cried Flint.

The British and Americans scattered behind the tank and fumbled for their rifles. Helmets were placed on and the jangle of ammo was heard as the men cocked their rifles. After a minute of silence, Commander Beckett, the American interrogator, threw his cigarette to one side and peered over from behind the tank.

"Can't see anything," he whispered whilst slowly resting his rifle on the hood of the Sherman.

BANG!

His helmet blasted off into the grass. Flint clenched his M1 Garand and prepared for a hopelessly outnumbered battle. Private Neville hissed over to his commander.

"Where'd it come from, sir?"

Just at that exact moment as Neville spoke, a voice echoed in the trees however, none had traced it; except Flint.

"Hit one," the muffled sound arose once again.

Hit one? thought Flint. *It's English. They were friendlies!*

He knew that he couldn't simply stagger into the open from out of cover as it might've been a German mispronouncing something by mistake but he swiftly devised a clever idea.

Yanking into his combat pack, he snatched out a 'clicker', which had attracted his attention on one of the bodies from a dead British paratrooper at Sword beach. It was a thumb sized golden object with various engravings scribbled across it.

Click.

Bravo Six turned their heads at the surprisingly high frequency sound.

Click. Click.

Two clicks had returned.

Indicating that the unknown incoming force were friendlies. Flint hollered, "Do not shoot! We're coming out!"

He stood up from the shadow and stepped into the light.

"Are you insane? Get down!" shrieked his entire squad. Even Nowak had a go at him in Polish.

"Duck, you crazy Englishman!"

A dozen dark green soldiers emerged from the treeline. Their clothes were rags, ripped and shot to pieces, and half of them had sustained violent injuries on their chests and faces. They wore burnt blue berets and had mud smeared all over their uniforms. Two were carried on bloodied stretches, each one having no legs.

A young eighteen-year-old limped up to Flint with an empty Bren LMG lazily hanging in his hands on the leather straps.

"You're lucky Nigel over there had one of those clickers," he spoke blankly in a traumatised, broken voice. "We were just about to chuck a grenade."

Nigel exhaustingly nodded his bald head.

"Flint Mitchell. Delta Company," he responded.

"Colonel Freddie Morrowton. 15th Scottish Division."

They shook hands.

"What happened to you guys? Looking pretty rough," asked Flint as he glanced at the groaning men on the stretchers.

"We were just patrolling the nearest village, Konigsfield. Just over there."

Morrowton took off his blue beret and pointed at a smoking, silent village across the plains. "A company of Germans ambushed us." He spat on the ground. "We had to abandon the wounded."

"Where's your sergeant?"

"Missing in action. That really bogged us off 'cause he had the field telephone last. We sat stranded for a couple minutes under fire. Anyways," Colonel Morrowton waved at the Americans, "we better get going; these poor lads aren't going to make it 'til morning."

He pointed at the moaning soldiers on the stretchers who still mustered the strength to hold a pistol in hand. The Scottish platoon trudged to the dull entrance of Dedenbach in a mess of mud and blood. They were mourned upon by their fellow divisions as they entered.

"What now, Flint?" Hayden asked as he kept an eye on the whispering treeline.

"We wait. Sergeant Brighton should have something good for us now." He nodded.

13 HOURS LATER
MANCHESTER, ENGLAND

"Father!"

Helena Hendrix opened the wooden cupboard. She brought out a neatly tucked-away and polished box and placed it gently on the decorated table. Around her, fragrances of lavender and rosemary potted the cupboards and enlightened the flowery room. Running a national herb company wasn't easy. Frequent bombings here at Manchester had severely disrupted her chain of supplies and never mind the fact her business partner was at war!

Outside, the ringing of bicycle bells and happy chatter of families had kept her mind off Hayden. She thought of her brother every day. Even the odd sunshine in spring had invited her mind keep to drift from valuable rest.

"Yes, dear?"

Her father, Edward, brushed down the stairs immaculately dressed with a complete suit. He was a bubbly, overweight man. He prided himself of the 'Good old days' back when he was a MP for the local council. Now he was just an aging man in his huge pension. Helena spoke up, "Have you switched off all the gas lights upstairs?"

"Yes."

"And then put the local—"

"Lampposts out? Yes, don't worry I've already done all that, dear," interrupted Edward, already knowing what she was going to say. "Those German airplanes won't see us tonight!"

"Oh, I thought you'd like to know, the home front radio broadcast is about to start," she announced. The old man looked delighted and neatly brushed the specs of dust from his tie. He added ecstatically in a triumphant voice,

"Pull up a chair then!"

Both daughter and father dragged back the oak chairs across the floorboards.

"Let's hope our boys have beaten back those buggers! I've had enough of these rations for now. Time for those blasted Botch to have some of their own!"

"Okay, okay. Shhhh." Helena laughed. It was just classic father. "Hayden's still out there, you know."

The old man's face dampened and he rubbed his wrinkled chin in a great disillusion of false hope.

"I know. Our prayers are with him, darling," he comforted sadly.

Helena switched the crackling radio on and checked for the right frequency. She closed her eyes unusually long and slowly tuned up the muffled volume.

"Good evening, ladies and gentlemen. This is the BBC at five, here to inform about all the current events around the globe."

Helena gulped as the familiar man's voice became live on air.

"Today, our young men, still courageously fight on in the pacific. They have retaken the Philippines in a daring assault against the crippling Japanese empire. An excellent result, many brave British men have been awarded for their honour and skill in battle. More of the pacific information will be discussed after this important briefing. In the west, the Royal British Army continues to dominate against the Germans in their own homeland. These chain of victories edge the world closer to an axis surrender and closer to peace…"

Father smiled as he stared through the glass window to the bustling, outside world. The muffled broadcaster continued.

"Our prime minister, Winston Churchill, has spoken out publicly on the daring efforts of our loyal soldiers against the Nazis. 'Progress has been incredible' he stated earlier in the House of Commons. As a nation, we fully back his every move in crushing what's left of the Third Reich.

"Moving on, breaking news have positively stated that Polish and French resistance fighters confirmed that the last stretch to central Germany will be costly and significant in casualties. Hitler has fortified every bridge crossing over the Rhine River and swears by his life that 'every man shall fight to the death no matter the consequences'. The first assault begins today on the Ludendorff Bridge. Good luck to you, the British 3rd Division and as the sun sets in western Germany, let this remain clear in the darkness. This country has an unpayable debt owed to such brave men. May God be with you..."

Helena's eyes were wide open and glistened with shining tears in the candlelight. It felt like a drum had thudded her heart.

"Hayden's part of the British 3rd Division. They're the ones charging against Ludendorff..."

She burst into tears. Her father comforted her, passing on a new box of fresh tissues and nodded his head slowly.

"It's okay. He's probably been through much worse anyway. I just hope he knows that if he does die, let him to do it with honour for this country..."

17 – The Last Flare

Yankee Six Four! Where are you? We've begun the invasion of Remagen! Heavy casualties and our tanks are already stuck in the bog! Get in here, over!

"Hold on a bit longer. This fine Sherman's on its last legs! They have no idea what's about to hit 'em!"

Bravo Six's final members sat on the dusty back of the American's Sherman tank. It grew into late dusk and the sun began to dive behind the invisible horizon, almost blinding itself from the world. Around them, looming grey trees fled by as the vehicle sped across the narrow forest road. Bleak darkness encircled and low branches frequently smacked into their camouflaged helmets. Only moonlight shone among them. It came showering down from the broad and vast skyline above, a multi-million gathering of lucid stars and lustrous galaxies. The white light empowered the soldiers as they bumped up and down the rocky path. Damp moss and unknown tree trunks surrounded loose shadows of forgotten caves and rippling waterfalls. It was calm, almost relaxing, but the engine of man-made machinery threatened perplexed nature.

The disturbance of booming and crackling emerged from the distance and combusted with the common wolves' howl. Flint dangled his legs off the tank and watched the lingering lights in the wilderness begin to reveal itself. The Sherman slipped out the last stretches of dense woodland and down a winding, dirt road. A tremendous view gazed upon Flint's lost eyes.

Ludendorff Bridge was shallowly sunk in between an almost valley-like effect. A slope of terrain curved up two ways. One mountain on one side and another on the opposite. An inferno of hellish shades twisted in between a bombed, shattered urban town. Remagen was sprawled along the nearest side of the river, with the Ludendorff entrance being at the river's banks. Bright lights and smothering flames engulfed what was left now of peace and an expansive amount of troops were seen scattered across the town's opening gate.

On the opposite side of the huge bridge, small concrete bunkers were placed at the exit. The machine gunners obliterated all the allied soldiers as they began a heavy haul of progressing through the miniature town. A contrast between mother nature and human suffering collided as Commander Beckett flattened his boot on the sturdy gas.

Flint panted heavily and his rifle nearly slipped out of his hand from the sweat. His knees were weak. Vision weary. A sudden disturbance, however, rid him off his ever-growing nerves.

"I'm gonna have to drop you off at the fields here!" a deep voice echoed from inside. "You have about two hundred metres to reach the foot of Remagen!"

Sergeant Brighton nodded and sternly drew back the handle on his Lee-Enfield. He glanced at his petrified squad as they swiftly loaded their rifles for the last time.

"Aaron! Why you looking so pale? It's a fine night out."

Aaron White smirked in response and inspected his barrel. Scott Addington, on the other hand, sat quietly on the corner of the Sherman, right above the fuming exhaust. His eyes were starry as he wrote the final notes in his blood-soaked diary. His fingers scribbled across the page as he connected with the moment. Brighton ignored him, rolling his eyes, and eyed the nearby chatters of gunfire.

"Sergeant? I thought we were the recon scouts! Why has an invasion started?" Flint gazed upon the flaming background and water's edge.

"I've told you this already, Mitchell. Since Nowak leaked their plans, high command has issued an all-out attack to hit their defences while they're still preparing."

"Ambush?"

"You could put it like that."

"Grass is coming up!" interrupted Hayden as he watched the field drawing in closer by the second.

At that moment, a squadron of veteran RAF fighter planes burst in from the smoking skyline, ammo filled and fuel containers full. Cheers were heard as their engines roared with fury as they spat bullets riddling at Remagen.

BOOM!

The leading fighter burst into a ball of melting iron and flames. A face of shock swept over the platoons as they realised the pilot had never parachuted out. The falling, and failing, plane ducked beneath the edge of the mountain and imploded into a cloud of fiery smoke.

"Out now!"

The cry from Hayden snatched Flint off guard and he was sent tumbling off the tank into the sodden grass. He clambered back up, but Scott barged him back into the wet mud again.

"Heads down!"

A stream of MG fire zipped over their heads.

"Cheers, mate!" Flint smirked.

"Crawl!" Brighton ordered as they slogged through the mud. "They got riflemen pinned on us!"

Flint felt his clothes soak in night dew but harnessed the power to carry on. They had to make it to the first row of houses!

Another terrifying explosion ripped out from the town's main gate. A shatter of shard and steel rained down upon the murky soldiers and the sky morphed into a mist of ember orange. The incoming fire halted.

"Their defensive towers are down! Go, push up!" a British scream pierced the crackles of loose gunfire.

Charlie Company had assisted the rest of the 3rd Division and came sprinting out the entanglement of clingy moss and grass. One hundred and fifty battle-hardened soldiers now had officially begun the assault whilst pacing down the fields. Bayonets had been fixed with the most brutal intentions. Sergeant Brighton, however, stayed down on the floor and rapidly connected his field telephone up to connect signal. Flint sprinted past, however came to a juddering halt as the sergeant sharply called him back.

"Flint, call in suppression fire for the infantry."

He wiped the mud of his cheeks and grabbed the telephone as if his life depended on it. The bullets were still flickering past.

"101st Airborne and 36th Sherman division, come in, over!"

"*Standing by, 3rd Infantry.*"

"Get us supporting fire on those houses! We're falling like flies here!"

It was a few halted seconds before the radioman crackled in again.

"Uh...negative, Bravo Six. We cannot engage until these Panzer tanks are dealt with up here in the forest. Over and out."

Brighton shook his head as he spotted flashes of cannons through the trees in the mountains. Flint continued desperately as he witnessed the British hammered into the night mud.

"101st?"

A Canadian accent rippled through the machine in a displeased tone.

"Enemy AA guns just shot down our planes! Our paratroopers have been scattered throughout Remagen and we're too spread out to join!"

Flint looked up at the lonely, disguised soldiers who burst out from the long strands of grass and moss.

"You tried. But it wasn't good enough. We're just going to have to keep moving," Brighton exclaimed as he clambered up. Flint shook his head in displeasure over Brighton's long-lasting sour tone against him.

Bravo Six dashed along the forsaken plain. Frequent bullets zipped beside them; however, no real firepower had been unleashed. The Shermans had made sure of that as they bolted shells into the village. The first house rushed up to about ten metres as the soldiers scattered out the grass and onwards.

Slip!

A small log tripped up Flint's boot and he slid into the grass. Trampled on by more allied soldiers, he witnessed the true power and toil of the invasion. Artillery shells bombarded the bunkers on the furthest end of bridge; tanks, both British and American, rumbled in from the forest and crushed fallen tree trunks. All supported by a hefty infantry assault.

Aaron, desperate to get to cover by the expression on his face, yanked Flint by the shoulders and heaved him up as he handed him back his dripping rifle. The sprint continued.

"First squad on me!"

A platoon of fresh soldiers filed up against the closest brick house prepared for an all-out close-quarters firefight. Grenades ticked and rifles loaded. Flint examined the empty windows in the surrounding houses and swiftly leaped over the long wooden gate. Bullets shattered into it just as he made contact with the ground. A sigh of relief came like a refreshing breeze as he staggered up. Grass morphed into dirt as he jogged over to the waving Brighton, back leaned against the corner of the first house.

"Scott!" The sergeant panted as he gazed back on the field they had just marauded through. "Get out your shotgun and give these animals a surprise!"

"My pleasure, sir!"

BANG! BANG! BANG!

Scott's Winchester blasted off the hinges and rocketed back the door. He retreated to the back end of the line as they breached in one by one.

Flint crept and felt the nervous sweat drip off his forehead onto his awaiting weapon. The squad were greeted with a dark yet silent single storey house. No Germans hid as Flint double-checked the room under the stairs, an ugly maggot infested bathroom. Guns still pinged and boomed outside on the street but Brighton spoke up, "Scott, is the dining room clear?"

Scott pivoted his head and commented, "Just like when it was built."

"Good. We're gonna take the back entrance and stay on the pavement up until the bridge starts. Mitchell, take point."

"You mean…we're heading right down the centre? Look at all them," Aaron moaned and pointed through the grimy window at the bullets as they splattered into the soldiers.

Brighton snapped back, "We did it back at Normandy, we can do it here…"

Flint picked up the light birch chair beside him and battered open the back door. Splinters of wood sparked into the ceiling and into his chest.

"All right Bravo Six, let's move." The snake of British soldiers once more winded through the rusty allotment of broken homes and wrecked sheds; the darkness strangling the air around them like a dying candle. Passing across the alleyway in a nick of time, they discovered themselves back in the thick of war again.

Lead flashed past as they piled behind a busted dumpster in instant reaction. Flint kneeled to the side and let his head and rifle hang out in the air of the exposed street. Through the iron sights, he caught track of a Germans' squad quickly making their way to a deserted AA gun. No longer. Two rapid bullets whistled across the road as a couple tumbled to the floor; one still crawling as he dragged his bleeding self behind a burning container.

"UPSTAIRS WINDOW!"

A flash and whisk of wind shredded through the village and blasted into the hood of an awaiting British Cromwell tank. Screams ripped out from the hull and echoed in the surrounding area. The tank had luckily not been destroyed, but all the crewmembers had been cluelessly incinerated inside. An officer in full SS black grinned whilst heaving another shell into his smoking Panzerfaust.

"You, over there!" Flint called as he ducked upon another trailing bullet skimming his leg.

The American soldier, kitted in a ghillie suit, looked up from his current posture, which was lying on a heap of library rubble motionlessly.

"Panzerfaust on the second floor - just by the lamppost!" Flint pointed at the gloom face in the dark. The sniper sprung back the ammo from his Springfield and manoeuvred slowly but carefully behind a dead German's body. He waited patiently.

BANG!

The sniper gun rocked back. Flint spotted the SS officer ragdoll out the window and onto the street, finished off with shots to the chest by the British next to him. With a clear opening now lying ahead, he burst out from behind the dumpster and covered his head from the MG fire that whizzed past his head.

"*Nein! Das ist einer!*"

A couple of German soldiers burst out from another brick house and drove shots at Flint. He skidded behind a broken horse cart, witnessing the lead pepper through the wood and root out into the field. Flint clenched his rifle, took a deep breath, and rocked over the sides to meet his enemy face to face. The first scurried towards him with a bayonet, screaming in German as he did so. Flint felt the curve of the cold metal trigger in his fingers and pulled. Two unstoppable bullets rocketed out and hit the running man in the chest and neck; crippling him to the concrete.

The second was cleverer, kneeling beside a wooden barrel and firing stray strands of lead in his general direction. Flint waited impatiently for his head to stick out once more, so that he could deliver a deadly dose of gunfire.

As planned, the grey-coated male sprung up, his shots narrowly missing Flint's face, before the Brit snapped a cold whizzing bullet through the damp night air. The German awkwardly twirled to the floor and stayed there, his helmet cracked and filling up in scarlet red.

"In here!"

Two Americans cried for help in a lone, steaming shell crater in the centre of the burning street. Flint leaped in and felt the dirt and rubble clog up his shoulder. The lamppost beside them creaked to the side and clobbered into the last sets of houses standing from the Rhine. The last axis soldiers wandered into the street and fought until the very end.

"Take 'em out!" the American shrieked behind him.

Flint obeyed and crawled out the crater into mists of black and yellow. The Germans dived for cover as quickly as they could, met in sight of an entire allied tank convoy battering through the street. It consisted of three medium tanks, two British Cromwells and one Sherman, a couple of jeeps with a .50 calibre gun stuck on the back. Hayden rushed up behind Flint and they both charged down on the hiding Germans.

BANG! BANG! BANG!

Flint whipped out his handgun and triple-shot the sobbing soldiers fighting on in the road. An infantryman burst out from the nearest shop door and scattered his MP40 fire towards the central of the convoy. Flint relentlessly dealt with him using the bullets in his M1 Garand. The German fell into a stack of hay next to the wall and his blood trickled into a drain.

"Remagen's clear!" the Americans celebrated. "Take the bridge!"

BOOM!

A dozen Germans burst out from the nearest bar in cries of anger and hatred. Their MP40s and rifles flashed at the British in the open. The two armoured jeeps parted from the moving line of vehicles and drove straight into them as they crashed into the brick walls. Smoke and flames funnelled to the sky from beneath the bonnet, a bad sign. As the axis soldiers limped back up and shot one of the drivers who quickly reversed, the truck skidded backwards, barrelling into a compact stack of flammable petrol bottles.

Upon seeing this, the second jeep watched as the Germans dared to escape...running for their lives down the road. Flint peered in pity as the MG gunner cut down the soldiers where they were. The retreating Germans tried one last counter-attack however too many of them were being hammered into the pavement.

Now with the road locked down and secure, the allied convoy bulldozed past Flint who took the time to sum up a breather behind a column of busted German munitions. Two British riflemen took position at the entry of the bridge and signalled for a sudden stop due to a hidden yet common trap.

Barbed wire.

They cut heaps of the defensive wire swiftly, fingers constantly pricked and cut under the immense strain they buckled under. Commander Beckett, exhausted and greasy, hurled his anger out from inside the vehicle, "Come on, already! We gotta get this armour on the bridge!"

The two soldiers looked up and worked even faster as they battled with the wire.

"We're tryin' our best, mate!"

Suddenly in an instant, they toppled over one another in a bloody mess of barbed wire and bullets. The bunkers lit both soldiers up and left them lifeless in the middle of the street.

"Alexander! Davis! Go!"

An Irish sergeant wailed out at his two youngest commandos as he peppered covering fire at the long distance bunkers. Alexander, short and skinny, burst out from behind the rubble and limped towards the unfinished work. He had already been shot once! On the other hand, from the opposite side of the road, Davis leaped over a row of German bodies and darted for it...only to be greeted with the faint sound of whistling in the wind.

BOOM!

A mortar shell blasted yards away and launched him up into the humble darkness. Alexander dashed over to the half-cut wire and grabbed the cable cutter, snipping at the tangle of spiked weapon. Holding a thumbs up, he finally clawed it loose and kicked it to the side. The convoy trundled forward with squeaking treads and advanced towards the start of the bridge on his signal. It was still facing scatters of small-arms fire from across the structure, however luckily, they were holding out well in strong formation. The original, main road led onto the bridge, a highway-like path over the forsaken water. The first tank, another British Cromwell, suddenly went over what was like a ramp and thudded back onto the concrete. Its whole engine shook and created a ringing vibration throughout the steel. The Sherman followed intensely as it fired lasers of bullets at the end of the bridge, not concentrating on the bump.

The lid flapped open on the Cromwell and terrified faces clambered out. Hands shaking. Rifles loaded. They leaped off the side and dashed for the nearest cover. The tank was left stranded in the centre of the lead-up road, completely abandoned.

"Hey!" Flint grabbed one of the crew by the arm and saw cuts and bruises battered against his weary face. "What's going on?"

"It's the Cromwell! We just hit a mine and it goes off in fifteen seconds!" he shrieked into his face as he ran off for safety. A sudden trio of bullets zipped through him; smashing him into the shop window with shards of glass shattering over. *Commander Beckett!* alerted Flint as he dashed over to the reversing Sherman. It was only a few metres from the detonated mine.

SMASH!

Howls of agony echoed in the Sherman as it ignited. A multi-flame of red and blue rocketed into the sky as iron chunks and concrete rained down around the sector of the village. No bodies could be seen. Only a mash-up of scrap metal and clogged smoke.

Realising the Cromwell had exploded too, Flint and the rest of the hundred men bolted straight into the fiery jaws of the bridge. The valley dipped in and the darkness grew thicker. He maintained the last bit of energy from his soot-covered legs and strode alongside the pavement of the structure. Hayden, Aaron, Scott and Sergeant Brighton also joined the charge as they battled to the exit.

The concrete-encased bunker opened fire like a lethal buzzsaw. Its scatters off whistling lead slammed into the remainder of the force. The soldiers, who heaved their kit along, toppled into the ground, fast or slow. Like a wild berserker, Flint sprayed his bullets towards the bunkers and leaped over a flipped and burning car. A sad sight endured his eyes as Heaton lay dead beside it. Sergeant Raymond kneeled silently by and slowly searched him. He was scavenging for ammo even with the bullets landing by his feet!

Heaton's hand was still clenched onto his knife despite that his heart had faded away. There was no time to mourn.

Flint fired the last of his rounds from behind Raymond and snatched the Thompson sub-machine gun up from Heaton's side. He locked the muddy magazines of ammo around his belt and re-accompanied his squad. They were hiding behind another flipped civilian motor. Its coal black paint melted and dripped onto the floor as the group reloaded their hot weapons.

"Scott! Get an RPG and hit that bunker on the left side."

"Yes, Sergeant!" Scott, limping and scarred, heaved the powerful weapon off his back and aimed carefully at the never-ending source of gunfire. His body rocketed back.

WHOOSH!

The cylinder of gunpowder whizzed through the booming battlefield and slammed into some nearby trees, its tips catching fire and the main tree itself cracking to the mud. Scott shouted phrases of anger and rapidly added another rocket into the barrel. "You got to be kidding me!"

Flint replied back with nothing, as he knew it would only fume Scott up even more. Instead, he helped and held the end of the weapon stable. Brighton chattered his Thompson at the bunkers and hollered out, "We haven't got time to screw up! Hur—"

A bright, eye-watering flash imploded in the night sky. Dazzling scarlet embers floated down in the calm rush of wind.

"Who sent up a flare?" Hayden spoke out.

"Bravo Six this is Delta Nine Eight! We're pinned down twenty metres from your position by the broken armoured car! We need your help!"

"We're comin' Delta Nine Eight. Hold in tight," Brighton replied into the telephone and switched it off. "You heard the man. Lock and load. We're going in."

Flint tore out the empty magazine and plunged in a new batch of fresh ammo. He wiped away the sweating strands of chestnut hair which fell over his forehead. Sergeant Brighton waited until the machine gunner's bullets zipped somewhere else, then full-forced dashed out of cover followed by his finest men. Still with RPG in hand, Scott was the last to expose himself and leaped over the stacks of dead and crawling bodies.

Flint bolted across the bridge. The flare still lingered in the air. Its sparks illuminated the entire battle and created a dark mist of red smothering the bridge, like a savage spray of doomed light. Multiple artillery bombardments boomed into the terrain however, none shook him; he had inherited the strength of pushing on no matter the consequences. A line of bullets pinged onto the floor next to him and dent into the nearby barrels ripping out a phenomenal explosion. The Nazis started to come into view behind the last barricade of sandbags on the bridge. An MG42 pumped rounds towards the Americans and British and shot the men besides him, the men slipping into his feet.

"The armoured car! There it is!" rejoiced Hayden. The soldiers saw it, rushed, and heard the moaning of a stranded platoon.

"Delta Nine Eight?"

Half a dozen speechless soldiers nodded and slumped against their car, almost lifeless; they slowly treated their wounds with infected bandages. The dead lay amongst them and even on them; one of which included the radioman.

"Scott, Aaron and Hayden. Get these men back to those line of sandbags!" Brighton pointed at the defensive point fifteen metres back under the intense firefights. "Flint, you and I are gonna hold down this position. Let's finish what Cole came to do."

A glisten in his eyes was replaced by a short snap of his pistol, the bullets cracking in and out the barrel and at the Germans hiding behind cover ten metres away. It was the first time that he had spoken of Cole since his death. It had cut a deep part in him, that's for sure.

"Scott! Take the gunner, I got the medic!" Hayden ordered as he flung the limp soldier onto his shoulders.

The armoured car pinged with lead ferociously as Hayden retreated in the open. Bullets whirred past his ear however he kept his stride forth and direct.

BOOM!

A gas canister erupted into a lethal fume of fire, its flames spitting out mercilessly onto the American infantry who, in fiery reaction, screamed and collapsed to the floor. Flint, witnessing this horror, mounted his Thompson on the hood of the steaming vehicle and sprayed lethal bolts into the Germans' bodies. They tried peeking over…however were met a face-full of bullets. The trio of Brits worked tirelessly on through the red mist supressed by Brighton and Flint. Their clothes were rags, helmets cracked yet their hope had not been broken.

A scatter of bullets whizzed over Flint's head as he ducked; it tore into the charging British behind and left them stranded and bleeding in the open. He raised his head over again and watched as a couple of Germans marched in fury out from behind the sandbags. Clenching his teeth in bitter hatred, Flint's rage burst.

RATATATATA!

The Germans dropped and pulled the trigger mid-air, firing rounds into the sky unintentionally.

Scott heaved another riflemen on his shoulder, the blood seeping into his chest. Whilst pacing past the barbed wire and flipped cars, he spotted a couple of soldiers once again exposed in the open.

"Aaron!" he brokenly called as he wandered towards him. Aaron strained the last survivor off his chest and pushed him into cover. "Go back to Sergeant; those downed men there need help."

Scott twisted out of cover however was held back firmly. Aaron, astonished, ranted into his face, "You go out there and you're a dead man!"

"Then I guess I'm gonna have to join my old squad mates," he replied with a quick wink. Aaron ducked from a zip of gunfire and stood speechlessly still.

Scott fired multiple shots at the bunkers and in response, they absolutely hailed down on him. Puffs of concrete shattered into the burning night sky as the bullets continued. He stumbled over to the duo who shrieked for a medic. It was one American and one British. Besides them, their squads lay dead by their boots. The American sprawled across the ripped bridge floor had been concussed by a hit to the helmet, whilst the British leaned over beside him loading a new magazine into his Lewis gun. Scott dashed over and yanked at the American's shoulder straps. Just as he pulled, an almighty shell cascaded yards next to them and debris whistled into their chests. The injured American fluttered through the air, almost like a helplessly flapping raven. He flew over the bridge's iron barriers and crashed into the icy waters below; a deep drop down. Scott rubbed the gunpowder out his eyes and staggered over to the terrified, mumbling Brit. Once again, he snatched at his shoulder straps, dragging him to the nearest wall of cover. A bullet smacked the Lewis gunner's shin and he cried in agony.

"Keep your head up, you're not dead yet!" Scott blurted out as he realised blood came smearing onto the road. A small barrier of sandbags alerted Scott and he pulled himself and the soldier to cover, glancing at the Americans yards away who tripped dead to the floor. The injured soldier held a hand over his leg trying to desperately stop the dark liquid from flowing over. Scott searched a nearby officer's bag; looking for any sort of bandage or stitches.

"Das ist einer hinter dem Sandsack!"

What was that?

The limp soldier struggled to one side for his Lewis gun as Scott addressed the bandages. He heard the hoofing of boots and checked his magazine for ammunition. Empty. Reaching into his blood-soaked trousers, he ripped out a razor knife and peeked over the sandbags.

BOOM!

His head slammed back. Helmet flung off. The knife tossed into the air. More blood sprayed over Scott as he aimed his shaking pistol at the leaping force.

BANG! BANG! BANG!

Several bullets thudded into Scott's chest. He stumbled and lay still in an eternity of pain. The red lingering smoke dissipated into an out-of-world white. A German stood over him with the bayonet's edge on his heart.

SLASH!

"SCOTT!"

Aaron slammed a brick against the floor and spotted the shouting German in his iron sights. He fired over a dozen times. The German stood still despite the shots. His Gewehr 98 dropped to the floor; leaving him still standing lame without any sense that he stood by the edge of the barrier. Aaron, who charged in fury, kicked him over the side.

SPLASH!

Aaron rushed towards Scott. He was already long gone and he knew it. The battle cries and the last charge had just erupted however; he heard nothing. His best friend had been killed.

Flint peered over to the kneeling Aaron from the opposite side of the bridge, his hands covering his face. *There was still a job to do, the dead are dead,* he thought without the slightest drop of grief. Flint realised how much he had changed from day one. A frail, young and incompetent boy who had set his sights on destroying the Nazi war machine. From those experiences, he learned…and that was certain. Now? Well, he was on track to morph into a man like Brighton. Knowing the trueness of battle and yet feel the bitter hatred descend upon him. It was fair to say that war had changed him.

Hayden stumbled towards them and opened fire.

"Scott's dead," Flint implied. A shocked expression flood Hayden's face and he ducked behind the car, for a moment, to himself. Flint chucked over a hand grenade and turned his head towards Brighton.

"Sergeant! We clear to move?"

"Yes," he alerted all the near soldiers who huddled around ditches and wild fires. "Move up!"

Flint streaked around the side of the armoured car into an exposed space, every inch covered by native German guns. However, none fired. All that could be heard was the longest chain of shooting that he'd endured. To his right, Hayden and Flint glanced at Aaron who strapped the MG42 across his shoulder.

RATATATATA!

"Go!" he screamed at Flint as the Germans ducked from his whizzing gunfire. He ferociously turned his rocking head and gazed upon his enemy. "I'm gonna kill every last one of you!"

With his support, a final charge mounted and pushed over into the exit of the bridge. The last Cromwell tank had re-joined and gunned down every approaching Nazi, their fiery Molotovs igniting in their hands. Flint leaped over the sandbags and peppered three Germans working a ground mortar. Without logical interference, he automatically dashed at another pair of Germans.

His Thompson's bullets sliced into the escaping Germans and their arms flayed into the air as they collapsed onto the grass. Brighton came up from behind and patted him on the back.

"Good…you're learning," he commented deeply.

Hayden crept up on a laying German sniper and slipped his knife out from his boot. He plunged it into him and swiftly snatched a Molotov from his pocket and a stack of grenades from his bag.

"Fire in the hole!" Hayden tossed all the explosives towards the dug-in enemy.

BOOM! BOOM! BOOM! CRACK!

Whilst the grenades let rip shatters of shrapnel, the Molotov spread an instant trail blaze. Some Germans leaped out from their cover to escape the steaming fire; but the helpless or unarmed ones were killed where they stood. The rest scurried for water and galloped to the river, not knowing a battalion of Canadian paratroopers lay perfectly still, waiting for them.

Aaron scampered further into Nazi territory, his fury and tragedy slowly depleting in the unusually lonely breeze. Soon, he dent in so far that he eventually broke away from the main attack and committed to a one-man rampage. His heavy machine gun suddenly stopped and steam funnelled out the barrel. It had overheated.

Slipping down behind a thick shrub of overgrown weeds, a few moments of rest indulged his comfort. He tried his best to fix the gun, coming to terms with his sudden rage, he realised that he had been utterly stupid to break off. Flashes of small-arms fire scraped past, but he had been lucky. The darkness here was severely intense and it was as if natural light had never existed. A single German private suddenly wandered in from beside him and gasped at the sight of the hiding man in the grass. Aaron whipped out his M1911 pistol and headshot him.

Breathe.

All safe.

Dink.

A small metal object clanged on the German's rifle and rolled down a slope into his boot. He looked down. A fused grenade met his strained eyes.

Run.

His helmet clattered off his head, but he kept running towards his comrades; screaming for help. He had forgotten his ammo, gun and combat pack, but luckily, he was out the firing line—

RATATATATATA!

There still remained twenty Germans in the main fight, however, they fought like a hundred. Until their last drop of breath had been obtained and their last drop of blood had been spilt; they constantly shot at the allies in random directions.

Flint and another American trio rushed a squad behind a burning combat truck, the eyes of the Germans wide open. Flint felt his bullets pound into them like sponge.

WHOOSH!

An RPG swept over, its familiar trail of smoke and dust following close behind. The two bunkers smashed open and crumbled to the floor in a mess of bricks and twisted wires. Cheering was heard as the MG42s or 'buzzsaws' had finally been demolished. A sigh of relief blanketed him.

Engines grumbled in from above Flint as he watched the last German fall from the bunkers then down the cliff. Before he could look, a whoosh of wicked wind swept Flint off his feet and cracked him into the windscreen of the idle combat truck.

"Messerschmitts!"

The undeniable dark grey underside of a fresh squadron of German Messerschmitts swooped along the tips of the dark oak trees in the distance. Their flares scattered into the empty forest as they expertly dodged incoming allied anti-aircraft fire.

"They're coming back around!" a wounded British colonel shrieked from his burnt stretcher.

The light faded. The shooting stopped. All eyes gazed upon the low flying fighter planes as they circled back.

Their machine guns riddled the bridge exit with ultimate fury. It just never stopped. The soldiers groaned in vast agony as they were hammered to the mud; fed up with last minute kills. However, just as they arrived, they left. Left into the German distance, retreating back to Berlin…

The job had been done.

The bridge captured.

The final battle victorious.

Even with the Germans' brutal last laugh effort, they still had been outwitted and outpowered. Flint Mitchell rolled off the hood of the bullet-ridden truck, thumping onto the mud below in a great deal of immense pain.

Something was wrong.

Sergeant Brighton, weary but pulling a scarred smiling, supported Flint to his feet. The strain, however, was too much and he collapsed back down to the dirt again. He sat limp against the wheel of the truck; near the German's he had just shot.

"It's okay, you're safe now. We're all going home..." Brighton quietly reassured as he looked at the glistening river. The sun emerged.

Flint looked around for one last time in slow motion. Aaron's body was dumped into the back of a long line of jeeps. Each having mountains of allied dead heaped on. The able survivors rested against the sandbags in smiles of joy and relief, rounding up the prisoners and ordering them to get in line. Hayden wandered over to Flint and knelt down.

"Hey, buddy." He put a hand on his shoulder. Flint tried to respond but he couldn't. All he could do was slowly nod and glimpse a scarred smile. Hayden's eyebrows narrowed as he realised there was no quick reply as usual.

"What's wrong with him?"

More than worried, he lifted the jacket off Flint and put a hand over his mouth. His normal army shirt revealed half a dozen bullet holes in his chest, all of which still bled with slow trickles.

"Why didn't you get him a medic!" Hayden rushed over to Flint's side and put a hand around his shoulder. Brighton stayed exactly where he was as he watched Flint's face get paler.

"Put him down. He won't make it to the medical bay," the sergeant painfully whispered.

"Medic!"

"Hayden..."

"What do you want! He could still live! Medic!"

The bloodied medics came scurrying in and set down the ripped stretcher. Their eyes were already gloomy and hopeless upon sight.

Flint Mitchell collapsed to the floor, his eyes weary as he smiled his last and leaned, perplexed, against the muddy truck tire.

His heart beat no more.

"Your death will not be in vain," Hayden Hendrix spoke proudly and buried his head in his hands.

William Brighton looked down to the dirt...

Many things played on Hayden's mind that day. Regret. Doubt. Hopelessness. But most importantly, revenge. He had never been alongside someone so brave; taken away in their final minutes.

"Goodbye, Flint."